EILISH MCGOVERN

ESCAPING THE HARSH REALITY OF THE IRISH POTATO FAMINE FOR A NEW LIFE IN VICTORIAN ENGLAND

BY

M. A. WRIGHT

Eilish McGovern
By M. A. Wright

This book was first published in Great Britain in paperback during May 2022.

The moral right of M. A. Wright is to be identified as the author of this work and has been asserted by her in accordance with the Copyright, Designs and Patents Act of 1988.

All rights are reserved, and no part of this book may be produced or utilized in any format, or by any means, electronic or mechanical, including photocopying, recording or by any information storage or retrieval system, without prior permission in writing from the publishers - Coast & Country/Ads2life. ads2life@btinternet.com

All rights reserved.

ISBN: 979-8821786043

Copyright © May 2022 M. A. Wright

For Nicola, this has been written especially for you knowing how you love this period of history. Hope you enjoy it.

Love Mum xx

Prologue

In 1845 when the Irish Potato Famine began, many were forced to leave Ireland and migrate to America and England. One such family was the McGovern's. Local farm worker Cormac, his wife Shelagh, and their two children, Eilish ten and Eamonn five, set out on their journey in April 1847 to England to find a better life. Many said Cormac was a fool to go, the famine wouldn't last for ever, but with both sets of parents dead, Cormac was not about to take any chances with his wife and children.

In truth, Cormac was worried about his decision to move, but with what little money they had, he felt the best way to use it was to book a passage to England and he would have enough left over to establish themselves before it ran out. He was sure he would be able to find work on a farm. He was a self-taught man and both he, Shelagh and Eilish were able to read, write and do simple sums, even Eamon was starting to learn, taught by his mother.

Cormac had plans for the family, he was determined not to be held back and when being employed by an English master, Cormac had listened intently to conversations not because he was being nosey but because it was the only way to learn the language of the Country he dreamed of going too for so long. Now, it was time. They could wait no longer, this is what he'd been saving for, although he had thought he'd be able to save more before taking their leave but needs must, they could wait no longer.

By 1849, the McGovern family had been living in the hamlet of Wynchampton, in the English county of Oxfordshire, for two years. Cormac had secured himself a job on the Estate of Lord Henry-Carmichael Fanshaw who had been impressed with this Irishman's knowledge of farming, his skill with livestock and the fact he took instruction and carried it out efficiently. If Lord Fanshaw had any concerns he would admit to feeling uneasy with the man's pride. It was almost an arrogance, not that Cormac was ever rude but there were times when he, Cormac, would offer an opinion unasked for, on something to do with the crops, or livestock, which when grudgingly tried, worked.

This annoyed Lord Fanshaw and the other farm hands, as he felt it showed that this Irish man, which is how he thought of Cormac, knew better than he or any of his other workers. This occasionally caused tension amongst the servants. Neither did it help when Lady Fanshaw favoured Shelagh for mending her fine clothes and underwear.

The other bone of contention was that Eilish went to the local school and could read and write better than many of the other children in her class. She was made fun of in the way she spoke so each night the family would sit round the fire in the winter or in the garden in the summer, practising speaking English without their Irish accents, no easy task, but they were determined as a family, to improve their lot.

Life was good for the McGovern's, they learnt to ignore the many nasty jibes said to them, as they went about their daily lives Cormac was happy, his decision to leave Ireland had paid off. Soon Eilish would leave school and seek work hopefully in one of the fashionable stores springing up in Oxford, then it would be Eamon's turn to go to school. Having to pay for schooling, Cormac could only afford one at a time. When Eilish went to work in Oxford, she would have to live in, several of the stores gave the young girls working for them, accommodation. Cormac was frugal with his money, so they would not need Eilish's.

As time passed and Lord Fanshaw got to know Cormac better, he changed his attitude towards the man, realising that it was not arrogance, but ambition that Cormac showed, and who amongst them could blame him for that.

There were of course, many of his social class who would disagree, but Lord Henry-Carmichael Fanshaw was not one of those. The world was changing, and would it not be better to employ educated workers on the Estate? Fanshaw thought it would.

His wife, though she favoured Shelagh McGovern's needlecraft, was not of the same opinion, still referring to the family as "Those bog Irish peasants." Though where she got the idea that she was so high and mighty, Henry was mystified. Had she forgotten that she herself was the daughter of a trader, a very wealthy one at that, and his desire to connect with aristocracy came when Henry's father almost lost Wynchampton Hall and the Estate, when he lost at poker to Lucinda's father.

Having no interest in the countryside, her father was quick to do a deal with Henry's father, and before he knew it, they were stood side by side in the tiny chapel on the estate, being joined together in matrimony.

Passionate about the Estate and knowing when his father died he could turn the estate around, Henry-Carmichael accepted his fate, and looking at the then pretty, quiet and what appeared to be sweet natured young girl, was happy to comply, if only to save the Estate. But that was all about to change.

Lord Fanshaw senior passed away six weeks later, and Lucinda turned into a lazy, scowling, quarrelsome young woman, who made not only the servants life a misery, but her husband's also. Three children later and Henry-Carmichael's life was a living hell.

hell.

CHAPTER 1

SEPTEMBER 1849

It was a lovely evening as Shelagh sat in the garden writing in her journal. She'd kept one ever since Cormac had taught her to write. She smiled to herself when she recalled how they'd met all those years ago when living in Ireland. She'd known of him it seemed like forever, but her parents had not encouraged the boy Cormac to their house despite feeling sorry for him as the boy had a dreadful home life. The McGovern's had lived in little more than a shack, and Cormac was the only child to survive out of the ten-given birth to by his mother. His father could never hold down a job, and when he was in work, all wages were spent on drink. He also had a reputation of being an abusive husband and father until the day sixteen-year-old Cormac had stood up to him and beat the living daylights out of the old man. Old man McGovern never lifted another finger to either his wife or son again, and when Cormac's mother died, his father followed six weeks later.

It was just after that, that Cormac had come across Shelagh one evening as she sat on a five-bar gate overlooking the field where he, then eighteen, had been rounding up the cows for the evening milking. Stopping to talk to her, they were soon walking out together, something that Shelagh's mother was not at all pleased about but surprisingly, her father was okay with. He'd pointed out how a young person's parent behaved, though disgraceful, should not be heaped upon the child, and from what he'd seen working on the same farm, the lad had promise.

Grudgingly, Shelagh's mother had allowed the friendship to continue, especially when her husband took ill and was unable to work, Cormac had often supplied them with milk, eggs and vegetables from his own small garden, where he'd kept a goat, half a dozen chickens and where after a long days work, he'd worked his small patch of garden, growing vegetables. The lad also taught himself to read, write, do some simple sums and could speak a smattering of English, though this latter achievement didn't always go down well with his neighbours. Like Cormac, Shelagh was also an only child and when her parents passed away, Cormac and Shelagh were married.

'Mammy, did you hear me?'

Shelagh was brought out of her reverie. 'Sorry Eilish, I was far away, what did you say?'

'I said where is Eamonn? Shouldn't he be home by now?'

'He went to help with the harvest, you know how he loves to be with your Daddy, and if he can pick up some of the spilt grain for me to use for bread, he feels he's really help..........' Shelagh got no further as the cries of her son alerted her.

'Mammy! Mammy!' the boy came running into the garden, his face and hands smeared with dirt and blood. He was sobbing hysterically, trying to tell them something but they couldn't make sense of what he was trying to say. Just as they were looking round for help, Carmel Byrne, a neighbour.
came running into the garden ringing her hands in anguish. Shelagh and Eilish froze in horror as their neighbour related the awful event that had just taken place. As Carmel relayed details of the accident, and news that Cormac McGovern was dead, Shelagh passed out.

Crushed by an angry bull who'd escaped and careered around the wheat field where the men and women were in the act of harvesting, Cormac had taken it upon himself to try and catch the beast and get it under control. He knew this animal and was not afraid of it, confident that the animal would respond to his coaxing. But it was not to be, the bull was totally out of control. Having trampled Cormac into the ground, breaking every bone in his body, it slowly turned and trotted unconcerned back from whence it had come.

The doctor was called but it was too late. Lord Fanshaw was called to the scene and was shocked at what he saw, sending immediately for the undertaker and ordered that Cormac should be covered up such was the distressful sight. Unlike many of the wealthy Estate owners, Lord Fanshaw had a healthy respect for all his employees and was known to be a good employer. He especially held Cormac in high regard, having had many a good conversation with the young Irishman.

So it was with great distress that as soon as he had arranged with the undertakers to place Cormac in a coffin at his expense, he had him taken to the chapel of rest, then set out to see the widow McGovern.

News, especially bad news travelled fast, particularly in small, hamlets like Wynchampton, so when his Lordship arrived at the McGovern's cottage, help, advice and sympathy were in full supply.

Henry-Carmichael was quick to take charge and having politely asked everyone to leave, sat down to talk to Mrs McGovern and her children who were distraught beyond words.

Seeing his Lordship standing in the main room of the cottage, brought about another shock to Shelagh, surely he hadn't come to tell them they had to leave the tide cottage which went with Cormac's job, but she was wrong.

'My dear Mrs McGovern, I cannot tell you how dreadful I feel that your husband.....has suffered such.........'

'What are we going to do? How can I go on without Cormac?' Shelagh cried out pitifully, the tears coursing down her face. Eilish was holding a sobbing Eamonn and at the same time trying to comfort her mother and biting her lip trying desperately to control her own emotion. Henry-Carmichael looked down at his feet. How could he look this woman in the eye. Although it was not his fault, he still felt a responsibility. Eventually, he looked up, shaking his head slowly. 'I'm so sorry. So deeply sorry. Cormac was a good man, a fine employee and one that will be sorely missed.' he said.

'Not half as he will be missed by us!' Eilish blurted out and breaking down uncontrollably. With great difficulty, Shelagh stood up and went to her children, taking them into her arms and holding them tightly. 'Hush now, hush. Rudeness will not help us now and neither will it bring your Daddy back. As their sobs subsided, Henry-Carmichael hung his head in sadness. Rarely had any of his employees died in such tragic circumstances he was almost lost to know what to do but do something he must and quickly. This little family would soon be wondering what kind of future they faced. As if reading his mind, Shelagh asked. 'What will happen to us Sir? He looked at the tear-stained face which already showed signs of fear of the unknown.

Henry-Carmichael pulled himself together, he had to reassure them, of what? 'Firstly, I can assure you, you will not be made homeless. This cottage will remain your home for as long as you want it.'

'But your Lordship, how on earth can we live? We have no money to live on and if you require rent............'

Henry-Carmichael held up his hand. 'The cottage came as part of Cormac's pay, I'm sure we can come to some arrangement. Perhaps we can find work for your daughter and your son. I know you have often taken in sewing and mending of my wife's garments, I know her Ladyship is particularly impressed with your needlework.'

'But Sir, my daughter is yet but twelve years of age and my son only seven.'

'Yes, well, I'm sure we can work something out, in the meantime, I want you to know that all costs appertaining to the funeral will be met by myself, it's the least I can do. Other arrangements can be sorted after we have laid the poor man to rest.'

'When....when can I see him?' Shelagh asked Henry-Carmichael who felt even worse now. How could he tell this poor young woman her husband had been so gravely injured he was unrecognisable.

'The undertakers do not recommend it.' he almost whispered, swallowing hard. Slowly he lifted his eyes to meet hers as the meaning of his words sank in.

Shelagh gripped her children once again, not wishing to breakdown and cause them further anguish. She would hang on and wait until she was in the safety of her bed, only then would she let go and grieve inconsolably for the man she loved, never to be held in those strong arms again, never again to be able to lean on him, knowing he was always there to keep the family safe. She was utterly bereft, and scared. What would become of them?

In bed that night, there was only one thought on Eilish's mind, apart from grieving the loss of her Daddy, it was the remark made by Lord Fanshaw about finding her work!

CHAPTER 2

The death of Cormac McGovern had reverberated far and wide, mainly because Cormac had not only been a well-respected man but secretly admired for the way he'd educated himself and his family. Cormac had high hopes especially for his family.

Eilish was almost twelve and he'd hope to keep her at the village school for at least one more year thereafter hoping that one day she would be able to apply for a position in one of the many department stores opening in Oxford, where they also provided accommodation. He had plans to send Eamonn to school as he could only afford to send one of his children at a time. As a family, they'd discussed all this and Eilish couldn't wait to go to Oxford though of course she would miss her family. Lord Fanshaw's remark about finding her work had worried her. Did he mean up at the Hall? Although she didn't look down on anyone in service, it was not a route she'd ever wanted to take and she knew, neither did her daddy. These thoughts she kept to herself knowing her mammy had enough to worry about. And what about Eamonn? He'd been taught at home by his parents but Eilish knew that as soon as she left school, her daddy planned to send him to the village school, again, service was not something he'd planed for Eamonn, he wanted him to learn a trade.

Lady Fanshaw had continued to send items from The Hall for Shelagh to mend and although she didn't feel like doing anything, grieving as she was, Shelagh also realised they needed the money. Cormac had been a good manager of money and so had Shelagh and after checking the biscuit tin that held their savings, Shelagh reluctantly told Eilish she would have to leave school immediately and there would be no chance of Eamonn following in her footsteps, instead Shelagh suggested that Eilish should take over Eamon's education while she, Shelagh tried to find extra work.

The funeral of Cormac McGovern took place ten days after the accident and there was a good turnout of the male population as it was seen as unseemly for women to attend these occasions.

When Henry-Carmichael informed his wife they were footing the bill for the funeral and he expected his sons Joseph and Teddy to accompany him, Lucinda was most put out and told her husband in no uncertain terms. At the same time, he also informed her that he was to offer Eilish, work in the kitchen. She was furious. 'I have no wish to employ ignorant Irish immigrants in MY household, whatever would our neighbours think? That we cannot afford English servants?'

'I'll have you know my dear that Eilish is not ignorant and is better educated than most of the below stairs servants, and may I also point out that it is *MY* household and it is *I* that employs them.'

'Mama's right!' butted in Mirabelle who at twelve was becoming quite the little madam.

Henry-Carmichael turned his steely gaze on his daughter his lips pursed as he looked thunderous. 'And you young lady should learn to be seen and not heard. My discussions with your Mama are nothing to do with you. How dare you interrupt me! Now, go to your room.' Mirabelle pouted and flounced out.

Much to the surprise of all who attended the funeral, Lord Fanshaw, paid tribute to Cormac. His sons, who'd returned from their boarding school looked around at the congregation. Joseph, the eldest at seventeen, looked hostile and arrogant, Teddy, twin brother of Mirabelle just looked bewildered.

At the end of the service, Lord Fanshaw shook hands with the vicar and everyone returned to their work. But Lord Henry-Carmichael Fanshaw had gone up in the estimation of everyone, agreeing that there were few landowners that would have done what he had.

Before returning to Wynchampton Hall, his Lordship had another visit to pay and one that couldn't wait.

When he arrived at the cottage, the front door was wide open though the curtains were drawn out of respect, it being Cormac's funeral. For late September it was still very warm. Knocking on the door and receiving no answer, he stepped inside calling out. 'Hello......hello, Mrs McGovern, is anybody there?' Suddenly a rustle of skirts could be heard as both Shelagh and Eilish rushed in from the garden, brushing the dirt from their Mourning clothes.

'Oh, your Lordship.' Shelagh gasped hurriedly wiping her hands on her apron. 'I'm sorry, I didn't hear you, we were out in the garden gathering vegetables.' she looked flustered and embarrassed and it made him smile but wished she didn't appear so scared of him. He couldn't help noticing that despite the hard life she led, she was still a beautiful woman and there was something so gentle and graceful about her, he couldn't help thinking what a lucky man Cormac had been. Although she spoke good English, she still retained a slight Irish lilt which he found oddly attractive. Pulling himself together when he noted that both mother and daughter were staring at him oddly, he coughed. 'Em, I'm sorry to intrude on you on such a sad day, but I wonder if I might talk to you for a moment. I hope you will forgive me for bringing this up on this day of all days.

'Oh, please, your Lordship, where are my manners. Please, take a seat, and would you like some refreshment? Tea, or I've just made some lemon barley water?' Shelagh said quickly pulling out a chair for him to sit down. Much of this was said to give her time to think. Why was he here? had he changed his mind about letting them stay? Where would they go? ' Sorry?' His Lordship had said something but she'd missed it, but Eilish hadn't.

'It's alright Mammy, I'll go, his Lordship said he'd have some of your lemon barley water.'

'Oh yes of course and bring some of those biscuits I made.' Turning to him she continued. 'Sorry Sir, it's been ....'she was about to say "one of those days" but instead, to her embarrassment, she burst into tears.

Henry-Carmichael was on his feet immediately, and putting a comforting arm round her shoulders, guiding her to sit in the opposite chair. 'I'm sure it's been a very harrowing time, especially today, which is why I've come. I wanted to put your mind at ease, especially where the future is concerned. I do hope I'm not speaking out of turn but Cormac was a valued worker and I admired what he'd achieved, having had to leave Ireland and his life growing up as a young lad. When I think of the privileges we've had, Lady Fanshaw, and my children, I sometimes wonder if they appreciate how lucky they are and how hard others have it?'

Shelagh dried her tears with her hanky looking surprised. 'My husband.......Cormac told you about....about his life?' Cormac had been such a proud, private man, yet here was his employer talking about Cormac as if he really knew him.

Henry-Carmichael smiled at her surprise and wished he could tell her to stop calling him "Your Lordship" and to call him Henry-Carmichael, but protocol would not have allowed it and the very suggestion would have horrified her, even smacked a suggestion of........'Oh yes Mrs McGovern, I was fascinated by Cormac's story, his life, his determination, his tenacity. I might be Lord Fanshaw of Wynchampton Hall, but all that came by a simple matter of birth right. I inherited everything, I didn't have to fight for it, yes I agree I have to keep many aspects in order, I give people employment, homes to live in, but..........' he held up his hands in a gesture of humble bewilderment.

Eilish poured a glass of barley water and gently pushed it towards him followed by a plate of the home-made biscuits Shelagh had asked her daughter to bring in.

Shelagh looked at this man, properly for the first time. What a lovely sincere man he was, so unlike the usual landowners, he must be one in a million. She felt so relaxed with him, She felt she could easily forget who he was and make a friend of him.

'You have nothing to apologise for Sir, we are all born in different circumstances and it is up to all of us to make the best of our lives. And, if I may be so bold to say, there are few Landlords that would have done what you have today, and for that I thank you, we thank you as a family for your kindness. Would it be alright if we visited my husband's grave later today, the children and I would like to place some flowers.'

'Of course.' he replied. Eilish went to leave the room, smiling her thanks. Eilish, don't go. What I have to say concerns you as well as your Mother.' Glancing curiously at her mother, Eilish resumed her seat. As I said immediately after the accident, you may remain here in this cottage, for as long as you like, but I appreciate the small amount of needlework required by my wife will not bring in sufficient for your needs. So I propose to offer Eilish work within the Hall. Unfortunately, due to her age, it can only be at the bottom of the rung, so to speak, but I can tell you that we will supply her with a uniform and six pound a year, paid quarterly. There would also be the offer of accommodation but seeing as you live so close you may wish Eilish to return home each evening, this would not be a problem and her wages would not be effected.' A look of horror was etched on Eilish's face forcing her mother to give her a quick kick under the table, as she did not want Lord Fanshaw to know this would be Eilish's worst nightmare, for he was only trying to help. The look had not escaped him and he knew from conversations with Cormac, that he and the family had better plans for Eilish. He continued quickly. 'Of course I know that this is not what you would have had in mind for your daughter. Cormac spoke to me about Eilish's desire to work in one of the department stores in Oxford.' He turned to look at Eilish and then her mother. 'And I can quite understand why, but at present you would be too young to be considered and in the meantime........well, I thought it might help, and of course there is no reason for you not to rise within the household servants as a vacancy becomes available and you become more acquainted with the workings of The Hall.'

'It's very kind of you Sir to think of us like this and we appreciate your offer, don't we Eilish?' Shelagh looked sternly at her daughter.

'Yes Sir, truly kind. What exactly would I have to do?'

'Well, it would be as a scullery maid for a time, but I'm sure with your intelligence, you will soon rise in the ranks.'

'Thank you Sir.' Eilish's heart had dropped to her boots. Though she did not consider the work beneath her, she just hungered for something more interesting.

'And of course when the time comes, and you are of age, I may be able to help you achieve your dream, as my wife and I are naturally acquainted with many of the store owners in Oxford.' He finished encouragingly. At this, Eilish brightened.

'Thank you Sir. It's very kind of you and I would be very grateful to accept.'

Shelagh let go a silent sigh of relief and at the same time, her pride in her daughter swelled. She knew that in her heart, Eilish's would be breaking but like her father, she was prepared to make the best of it until her dream could come true.

Then Lord Fanshaw dropped another surprise in their laps, one that initially caused some concern for Shelagh.

'Em, there is one other item I need to talk to you about, and this is something I'd like to discuss with your Mother in private if you will forgive me Eilish.' Eilish left the room, thanking Henry-Carmichael once again and wondering what on earth he had to say to her mother that couldn't be said in front of her.

'I hope you will forgive me Mrs McGovern, but what I have to say concerns your son, Eamonn. I understand that Cormac had plans to send him to school as soon as Eilish finished her education, and I realise that now this would probably not be possible. I would like, and this must be strictly private between you and myself, to fund the boy's education at the village school.' Shelagh gasped and a hand flew to her mouth, shocked at such a suggestion, just what did his Lordship expect in return? With Eilish up at the Hall each day and Eamonn at school, she would be alone in the cottage! Just what had he in mind? Terror shot through her. Lord Fanshaw saw the look on her face and realised to his horror that his offer had been completely misconstrued.

' Mrs McGovern! Please don't misunderstand me, my offer is without any obligation, it is given because of what Cormac told me and the fact that I know the boy already can read, write and do his numbers. I know he has a keen interest in the horses up at The Hall, and I did think that in the future, he would be a great asset to my stables. It is in my interest as well as his that he continue his education. This is precisely why it must be a secret between our two parties, where the money has come from to pay for his schooling. I will add it to the payments when settling my wife's needlework bills, so only you and I will know.' Because he was so horrified that Shelagh had thought he had a proposition in mind, it was now her turn to apologise for her assumption.

With a sigh of relief, and a smile, she shyly made her apology. 'Now it is my turn to apologise Lord Fanshaw, please forgive me for jumping to such horrible conclusions, it was unforgivable.'

'Nothing to forgive my dear. A widow in your position, of course you should be wary. Now, I must take my leave and let you get on. Thank you for the refreshment. I will inform my housekeeper Mrs Green, that she will have a new scullery maid on Monday. Normally Eilish would start at six each morning but as it will be her first day, please tell her to arrive at eight.'

Now all he had to do was inform his wife they were to have a new scullery maid, on second thoughts he decided to say nothing, least said soonest mended. As to Eamon's village school fees, she would have no need to be any the wiser.

CHAPTER 3

Eilish had been working at Wynchampton Hall for almost four months before it was discovered by Lady Fanshaw.

The first day had filled Eilish with trepidation. Mrs Green had been told to expect her and whose daughter she was. Lord Fanshaw impressed upon her that he expected Eilish to be treated like any other member of servants and did not want to hear of any derogatory remarks because of where she'd come from. If Irish workers could work on the land, he told her, they could also work at The Hall. The look he gave her said that he would brook no arguments and Mrs Green replied, 'Yes your Lordship' When he added, 'There's no need to discuss this with her Ladyship, it is of no matter to either of you, I say who works here and who doesn't.' His meaning was loud and clear, she was to keep her lip buttoned if she wanted to keep her job, though what she would say to her Mistress when she did find out! Lord knows.

Eilish soon picked up the routine. She was a quick learner and having been used to helping her mother around the home, she took pride in a job well done. There were twenty-four, servants, which included two scullery maids, one of which was Eilish, three parlour maids, one Lady's maid, a governess to Mirabelle, the cook and her assistant, Mrs Green, the housekeeper, the butler, Harold Stanley, and three footmen. The rest were outside servants, grooms, coachmen and gardeners, but they never ventured into the kitchen.

At first, most of the servants had been friendly towards Eilish but as they got to know her and realised how clever she was, certain members became aloof with her. This hurt her but her mother said, 'Ignore them, they're jealous because of your learning,' Strangely, it was those who you should have known better, who were the meanest. One of the biggest culprits was the butler who would make nasty jibes about the Irish when they were sitting round the servants room table having their meals. Eilish would ignore his remarks and the sniggers of the servants, though she often blushed with embarrassment.

One day he began talking about the "Bogs of Ireland" and how the whole of Ireland stank of pigs, and wherever you walked, you'd get covered in muck. Eilish had heard enough. Placing her knife and fork down, she slowly turned to look straight at the butler, staring at him until each member of servants noticed and went silent. Suddenly he realised no one was talking and looked up to see everyone staring at Eilish, who was glaring intently at him. He smirked, at last, he'd goaded the girl into retaliation. This was where he could show them all how one word from him to his Lordship, and she'd be down the road with her tails between her legs. 'Well girl! What are you looking at? Get on with your food!' You could have heard a pin drop as Eilish sat up straight. In a quiet, polite voice that she knew would anger him even more, Eilish asked. 'You seem to know an Ireland that I don't, please, could you tell us where this Ireland is, what part? Is it in the South or the North?'

You could see the rage building in him. Eilish continued. 'I take it you do know the difference. Could you perhaps tell us which side Belfast is on and where the Shannon runs and perhaps where the mountains and valleys are? the beautiful landscapes like those of the highlands of Scotland and the North and South of Wales, despite the coal mining areas.

'Be quiet!' he roared, banging his fist on the table which made everyone jump. Far from showing her up, he'd shown himself up as this chit of a girl seem to have more knowledge of geography than he. 'How dare you come out with such rubbish....'

'Oh it's not rubbish Sir.' she interrupted. 'This is a fact. Apart from my own knowledge at having grown up in Ireland, my father taught me about the rest of the world. You haven't told me when you went to in Ireland or where it was you saw what you earlier described?' Eilish knew she was now being impudent but she didn't care, she'd teach this pompous, ignorant man to poke fun at her and her beloved Country.

'Enough!' he roared again, apoplectic with rage. 'Leave the table! NOW!'

'But Sir?' Eilish retaliated as if mystified, though she was hard put not smile at the man's rage.

'I said leave the table NOW!'

Eilish looked round the table and slowly, unconcerned got up to leave. As she reached the door he barked. 'Don't leave this house until his Lordship has spoken to you.'

Without saying another word, she went back to the scullery to continue washing up.

At the table, nobody spoke another word. When the butler left, everyone had some comment to make but when cook made her comment.

'About time someone put that little minx in her place, far too big for her boots if you ask me, all that learning's made her think she's better than us.....' Mrs Green intervened.

'Well I think you would be wise to keep your thoughts to yourself, Cook.' Mrs Green remarked as she got up from the table. 'And that goes for the rest of you.' she said giving them each a warning look, as she left the room.

As she made her way back to her sitting room, she contemplated whether to have a word with the butler, warning him to tread carefully, after all to be fair, he had been goading the girl for months not that it was any excuse for her behaviour, but even Mrs Green was surprised at the depth of the girls knowledge. She'd just sat down, about to have her afternoon nap, when there was a knock on the door. 'Come in'

'Ah, Mrs Green, I hope I'm not disturbing you.' Mr Stanley, the butler said as he hovered in the doorway.

'Mr Stanley, come in, take a seat what can I do for you?'

'Well first I must apologise for losing my temper at lunchtime but that girl, whatever possessed his Lordship to engage her? We've never had Irish servants in the house, it really does lower the tone.'

'Mr Stanley, I think I should stop you there and give you a friendly word of warning. When his Lordship told me to expect her, he also warned me that Eilish, such a silly name, should not be treated any differently to any other member of servants. He also added "if they want to keep their job" I quote, his words not mine. So you see, if you do report her, which I have a mind that is your intention, I advise you to think carefully.'

Harold Stanley thought about this. He frowned. 'I don't understand, why should an Irish scullery maid be of any importance to his Lordship?'

Mrs Green wrestled with herself as to how much she should reveal. 'Well between you and me, and this must go no further, Eilish is the daughter of that Irish farm hand who got himself killed a few months ago.'

'Of course! That's why she doesn't live in. And her mother's keeping the cottage! Well, well, well. Do you think her Ladyship is aware all this?' Mrs Green shrugged.

'Who knows. All I know is, I'm saying nowt!' And as he left her room she muttered, 'And I advise you to do the same.' But Harold Stanley had other ideas.

Harold was unable to get her Ladyship on her own for the rest of the day and although Eilish waited, having been told not to leave until his Lordship had seen her, eventually she was told by cook, who'd been told by the butler, she could go home.

Nothing was said over the next couple of days and just as Eilish thought she'd got away with not being reported, Lady Fanshaw's maid came down to the kitchen one morning and told her to put on a clean apron and present herself to Lady Fanshaw in her private sitting room. Not knowing where that was, she looked about her in dismay. 'I'll show you.' boomed the voice of the butler. 'Follow me.' And without waiting he turned and walked swiftly up the stairs and through the green baize door which separated upstairs from downstairs.

Eilish had to run to keep up with him and nearly collided into him when he stopped abruptly outside a door, knocking and waiting until a voice bid him enter. Stepping aside he announced her. 'The Irish girl your Ladyship.' at which point he poked Eilish in the back so fiercely she almost tripped as she stumbled forward.

It took a few minutes for Eilish to take in her surroundings. The room was hot and stuffy, true it was almost February, and outside snow lay on the ground, but the heat was stifling.

The room was full of ….stuff. Everywhere, every nook and cranny, every shelf, even on the occasional tables there were trinkets of every kind. How on earth were the maids ever expected to keep the place clean, it must take ages Eilish thought.

'When you've finished being nosey and seeking your fill of my sitting room, perhaps you could explain your appalling behaviour in the servants quarters three days ago?'

Eilish turned her attention to Lady Fanshaw. She wasn't sure what she expected but she certainly hadn't expected such hostility. Lady Fanshaw was quite a large woman, her face looked swollen, her skin blotchy and her eyes seemed to disappear in the flesh surrounding them. In short she was the most unattractive woman Eilish had ever seen. 'Cat got your tongue?'

'Pardon?'

'Pardon your Ladyship! Have you no manners?' the woman sneered at her. Eilish could not understand why she was being so nasty.

'I'll ask you again, explain your recent behaviour at luncheon in the servants hall and the way you spoke to Mr Stanley?'

'I'm sorry your Ladyship, but it was he that was rude to me telling lies about my Country, I only asked when he'd visited Ireland and what part, that he was able to make such incorrect descriptions.'

Lucinda Fanshaw was amazed at the girls confident reply. She was addressing her as if she were her equal. 'What's your name?'

'Eilish, your Ladyship.'

'Eilish! What kind of a name is that?' she spat

'It's Irish.' Eilish explained

'Well I'm aware of that! It's a ridiculous name. Does it have an English translation?'

'I believe so your Ladyship, I think its Alice in English.'

'Then from now on you will be known as Alice while you're in this house. Now get back to the kitchen.'

'But your Ladyship.....' Eilish protested

'How dare you answer me back, get out of my sight or you can get back to the hovel you came from and not return, I shall be having words with my husband.'

Eilish thought it best to do as she was told, there was no talking to this horrible woman

Outside in the hallway, Harold Stanley was waiting for her. He had obviously heard all that was said. He smirked at her saying. 'You've got off lightly so far but wait till Madam speaks to his Lordship. I think your days are numbered, Irish!' Eilish decided his offensiveness was not worth a reply. If she had overstepped the mark, she didn't care. She hated the work here and hated the back biting and bullying that went on. When they reached the kitchen there was yet another humiliation for her to swallow. The butler clapped his hands, calling for attention. What now thought Eilish.

'Attention everybody. Lady Fanshaw wishes it to be known that from now on, Irish here, is to be known, and answer to the name of Alice. Now get back to your work, Alice.'

When Eilish returned home that evening and told her mother what had happened, she felt so sorry for her daughter that she should have to put up with such humiliation from a man that should have known better. How she wished she could take her away from Wynchampton Hall and keep her at home until she was old enough to apply to the department stores in Oxford. But Eilish had decided, she would refuse to answer to any name but her own.

It would be another two weeks before Henry-Carmichael found out that his wife was now aware of his employment of Eilish.

'Mama says the Irish girl is to be called Alice from now on.' Mirabelle announced one afternoon. Lucinda was resting on the chaise-lounge and Henry-Carmichael was reading his newspaper. It didn't immediately register with him until he looked up and saw his wife glaring at their daughter.

'What did you say?' he asked her

'She's making mischief as usual, take no notice. Mirabelle go to the nursery, Miss Pinkerton will be waiting for you.'

'But Mama.....'

'I said GO!'

'No wait.' Her father intervened. 'What did you mean? And don't call her Irish, her name's Eilish.'

'Not any more it isn't, Mama said.....'

'Enough!' her mother screamed at her and Mirabelle burst into well practised tears.

Henry-Carmichael looked sternly from one to the other then quietly said. 'Do as your mother said, go to the nursery, you must have lessons to learn.' As soon as she'd left the room he turned to his wife. 'Would you care to explain what our daughter has stated? And don't try fobbing me off with any of your lies.' he said as she was about to deliver some excuse.

'Alright then, I'll tell you. Though how you have the affront to take the moral high ground with me, when you deliberately set out to deceive me! I'll never know. The girl was causing trouble in the kitchen, deliberately answering back to Stanley of all people, trying to humiliate him. I told you I didn't want any Irish peasants in my household.......'

'And I told you this is My household and I employ who I think is worthy of employment!' He roared. Lucinda lay back frightened. It was rare for Henry-Carmichael to raise his voice, so when he did, you knew you were in big trouble. She realised she would have to get out of this sticky situation as soon as possible, and there was only one way out, blame someone else, and who better than Harold Stanley himself, after all, hadn't he been the one to start all this.

'I'm sorry Henry.' she cried pitifully into a handkerchief, 'Please don't shout like that, you know my nerves can't take it, it's my heart you know.' she made great play by placing her hand over her heart.

'Then I suggest you explain yourself Madam.'

'It was the butler, he came to see me, he was in such distress, threatened to leave.' she lied 'Said the girl was always trying to show him and the other servants up with her so called knowledge, made them all uncomfortable.'

Henry-Carmichael stared at her, his lips gripped tight in anger. 'Threatened to leave did he? Well, if he feels he should have some say in who works here, perhaps it is time he does leave.' Getting up, he stormed out of the drawing room and made for his study where he rung for one of the parlour maids instructing her to send Stanley to him immediately.

Poppy Lawson was more than happy to deliver this instruction. Like most of the below stairs servants, she was scared of Harold Stanley who was a cruel, bully so she couldn't wait to let him know the Masters mood. As they were all aware, Stanley had been the one who'd sneaked in to report poor Eilish to her Ladyship. Knocking on the butlers door, she opened it when called to enter. 'Please Sir, Master wants you in his study, immediately he said, seems in a terrible angry mood.' she volunteered and was pleased to see the smile previously on Stanley's face fade and a blanched look of fear replacing it. She turned and hurried out, not wanting him to have a go at her for what he might call insolence.

When he returned some half an hour later, Harold Stanley was very subdued and remained so for the rest of the day. This was followed by a visit from Lord Fanshaw when the servants were assembled for their evening meal, after their Master and the family had been served theirs.

Everyone respectfully stood as he entered. 'Please, be seated. I do not wish to interrupt your meal. I just wish to inform you, that it has come to my attention, that a certain amount of mischief has been made regarding a member of servants. I wish to make it clear that I pay the wages of the servants and I expect you all to work together in harmony and respect each other no matter what your status. Some of you receive higher wages than others, this is due to your age, experience and responsibility of the position you hold, it is not that you are superior. Every member of servants will be known by the name they were born with, and proud of it, there will be no name changing or calling here. Should any of you feel that you are superior and it gives you the right to torment another, please see me and we can discuss when you would like to leave and seek employment elsewhere! Good evening.' And he was gone.

For a moment everyone sat as if they'd been turned to stone.

'Well that's told us!' Cook muttered under her breath as she nodded towards the two scullery maids Eilish and Daisy, to start clearing the table. Harold Stanley suddenly stood up, scraping back his chair. 'I will not require pudding, Cook, I'm not feeling well and shall go to my room.' And with that, he walked out.

'Well!' exclaimed Cook 'I've never seen such bad manners! What an example to show these youngsters. Don't any of you ever do such a thing. Leaving when everyone is still at table is disgraceful if I say so myself, and I'm surprised.....'

Mrs Green, the housekeeper interrupted, she didn't want Cook's ranting to become yet more gossip. 'Yes, well, I think Mr Stanley has been under some pressure recently....'

'It's of 'is own makin'' Cook retorted

'That's as maybe but I think enough has been said and the subject should now be closed. As his Lordship said, he wants a harmonious servants. Now Poppy, Gertrude, will you please bring the delicious plum crumble and custard to the table.'

When Eilish returned home that night and told her mother what had happened, part of her was elated that Mr Stanley had been put in his place, but then she worried that it was because of her that he'd got into trouble. She thought maybe the servants would retaliate. She needn't have worried, far from retaliating most of the servants were elated that old Stanley had been brought down a peg or two. All except Cook and Mrs Green who secretly wondered just what it was about this Irish girl that the Master appeared to want to protect. ? Was it because her father had been killed on the Master's land or did he have some other ulterior motive. After all, they said in the privacy of Mrs Green's sitting room over a glass of Sherry, it was well known that the Mistress had let herself go, and there was no love lost between her and the Master, especially since they now had separate bedrooms. And, Cook pointed out, she had heard that the widow McGovern was considered an attractive, gentle soul, for an Irish, Cook would add scathingly. Eyebrows were raised shoulders heaved in big sighs, then Mrs Green sensibly changed the subject.

CHAPTER 4

For the next couple of years nothing eventful took place at Wynchampton Hall. At fourteen Eilish was promoted to parlour maid when Maisie left to get married. Since the debacle with the butler, Poppy and Eilish had become good friends and Eilish, to Poppy's delight, had been teaching her to read, write and do simple numbers. In return for this, Poppy was more than happy to show Eilish the ropes of being a parlour maid. They kept Poppy's learning a secret, as Eilish was scared of the others finding out and accusing her of showing off.

Now, as a parlour maid, there were occasions when she ran into the offspring of his Lordship. The eldest, a son Joseph, and his younger sister Mirabelle, were obnoxious, spoilt and ill mannered. Mirabelle still had a governess, Miss Pinkerton, but Joseph and Mirabelle's twin brother, were away at school during term time, which Eilish noticed was when she was left alone. It seemed Mirabelle liked an audience to her teasing and would encourage Joseph, who would have ignored Eilish had Mirabelle not encouraged him. Teddy on the other hand, was a sweet boy and as they were of a same age, he would often chat to Eilish, asking about Ireland, fascinated by her stories and secretly loving the Irish lilt in her voice. Most of the time, Eilish was able to avoid her Mistress but on the rare occasion when her Ladyship entered a room where Eilish was, she would glare at her with such venom that Eilish would make a quick exit. Since the day the butler had reported Eilish and Lady Fanshaw had hauled her over the coals, the woman never spoke to her, which always surprised Eilish.

On even rarer occasions when Eilish bumped into his Lordship, he would always pass the time of day, asking after her mother, and Eamonn, and although she appreciated his concern for her family, she was wary about being overheard by other servants, who might take it out on her, accusing her of favouritism, or worse. She was not deaf and had occasionally overheard snippets of conversation linking her mother's name with that of his Lordship, which she found upsetting, and offensive, although those talking would quickly change the subject when she was within earshot.

When she reached sixteen, Eilish began to wonder if she would ever get away from service and achieve her dream of working in one of the large department stores in Oxford. She would often talk to her Mother about this, asking if she could not speak to his Lordship the next time he visited to collect or deliver required sewing, but Shelagh said, not yet she must be patient for just a little longer. Wait another year she advised her daughter, Eilish groaned, but knew her mother had good reason to say this. Next year, she would be seventeen and Eamonn twelve, and Lord Fanshaw had promised Eamonn employment in the stables. Another year, how would she survive the boredom of housework.

Below stairs, life went on the same. The Fanshaw's were not one for lavish entertaining, although there were a smattering of dinner parties, mainly connected to Lord Fanshaw's Estate business. Lady Fanshaw spent more and more time 'resting' often not getting out of bed until mid-day.

Joseph had left boarding school at eighteen, much to the relief of the servants there and had managed to get into Oxford University, but as the tutors said, "money talks" now at the age of twenty-one, he was having to stay on as he'd managed to flunk all his exams due to the fact he rarely attended lectures and those he did, he'd slept through usually nursing a hangover. Only his father's money kept him from being thrown out in disgrace.

Teddy had also been sent to boarding school at eight years of age and had a terrible time as he was bullied mercilessly. He was a sensitive boy, kind and gentle and despite the bullying he never complained. Nor did he complain when he became ill and it wasn't until he collapsed on the rugby field and taken to the sick room, that they realised he was seriously ill. A doctor was called and Teddy was rushed to the Royal Infirmary.

As Teddy's fever rose out of control, Henry-Carmichael sat by his son's bed, day and night. When asked if she would like to join her husband by their son's bedside, Lady Fanshaw replied. 'Goodness me no, I'm sure Teddy will be as right as rain in a few days, he's probably making a fuss just to get out of school for a few days.' Nothing could have been further from the truth, as Teddy was known to be a good and enthusiastic scholar, and the school had high hopes for his entry into University.

When Teddy had complained he was unable to move his legs alarm bells rang, and specialists were sent from London's Harley Street. They gravely examined him, conferring with each other in low whispers. Eventually, they faced Lord Fanshaw with the tragic news, Teddy had contracted Poliomyelitis, a dreadful disease for which there was no cure and if it didn't kill you, it left you crippled for life.

The news when it hit Wynchampton Hall was devastating, The female servants wept, and the males amongst them, looked sombre. Lord Fanshaw searched the medical profession for answers, but there were none to be had. Lady Fanshaw's reaction silently angered the servants. Her cool, callous, dismissal of her son's illness, beggared belief.

After six months in hospital, Teddy was sent home, there was no more that could be done for him. But Teddy was not ready to be discarded as bed ridden. Lord Fanshaw had heard of a man who was experimenting with something he called "leg irons". He'd seen these items in a medical Journal and took the opportunity to speak to the Blacksmith that came regularly to shoe his horses.

'Can you make something like this? He asked him

Joe Blackstone rubbed at his unshaven chin. Yes he could make them, but how well young Master Teddy would cope with them was another matter. They would be heavy, and Joe didn't see how he would be able to move with them on.

'He has crutches.' Lord Fanshaw told him. 'To support his upper body.'

Joe shook his head uncertainly. He wanted to help but didn't think his Lordship had any idea of the task he was setting Joe, or his son. Joe wanted to help but was at a loss, instead, he suggested he would see Master Teddy and talk to him, but he would not make any promises.

Not long after returning home, Eilish found she was often the one to take Master Teddy's meals to him. It seemed that his father was his only visitor. Occasionally Mirabelle would visit but would soon become bored with him and in an effort to put some spark into him, would resort to spiteful jibes which just sent the poor lad spiralling into a depression, Mirabelle would then flounce out, leaving the poor lad devastated.

It was on one of these occasions that she collided with Eilish bringing his lunch. 'Oh here's Irish, I'm sure she'll have something clever to say. Go on in Bog woman!' Instead of being annoyed, Eilish muttered under her breath. 'Certainly pasty dumpling' and giggled when she realised that Teddy had heard her. Luckily, he giggled too. 'Now that's the first time I've seen you laugh since you came out of hospital Master Teddy.' Eilish said brightly.

Teddy stopped laughing and replied, 'Not had much to laugh about have I Eilish?'

Eilish put down the tray on the side table and helped him into a sitting position, then handed him the tray. 'Well now, what would you rather be doing?'

I'd rather be at school studying for my exams. Another two years and I should have been going to Oxford, now that's all gone.'

'Why has it?' Eilish spoke more sharply than she'd intended.

Teddy dropped his spoon with a clatter on the tray. 'Well why do you think?' he asked her angrily 'Has it escaped your attention that I'm a cripple, I'm unable to walk?' He stormed at her.

'No Master Teddy it has not escaped my attention and I'm neither blind nor stupid and I would thank you not to shout at me!' Eilish stood with her hands on hips and stared at him. Teddy opened his mouth to say something but nothing came out, he was so shocked that Eilish would speak so to him. 'And now you're going to say, "Do you know who you are talking too" in a posh voice, and I shall reply, " Yes Sir and do you know I'm Irish!" Suddenly they both burst out laughing.

'Oh Eilish what's that got to do with anything? You being Irish.'

Eilish shrugged and a big grin spread across her face. 'No idea, but it made you laugh, didn't it?'

'It certainly did. Oh Eilish, promise not to ever leave us, you are such a tonic. I could spend hours talking to you but I know you have work to do.'

'Well that's true, but there are times when I could sneak up here and keep you company. But Master Teddy, forgive me for speaking out of turn, but it's only your legs that don't work, you haven't lost the use of your brain or your hands. There is no reason why you shouldn't study and get to University.'

'Well passing the exams would not be impossible, but how do you suggest I get there and to and from the lectures?'

'On your crutches.'

'They hurt under my arms.'

'Where? Let me see?'

Teddy hesitated. 'Really, I can't show you.'

'Why not?'

'Well, I'm a man and you're a woman.' he said wriggling in the bed uncomfortably

'No! Really? Shock, horror. I had no idea.' Eilish held a hand to her mouth acting out a scandalised woman which again had Teddy in fits of laughter. And that is how his sister Mirabelle found them and she was furious at their familiarity with each other. How dare Irish behave like this in her brother's sick room.

'What's going on in here? What do you think you're playing at?' She stormed

'I was just bringing Master Teddy's lunch to him.' Eilish replied

'And taking advantage of a sick boy!' Mirabelle screamed at her.

'Hey, hang on sister, Eilish was making me laugh, I could do with someone to cheer me up.'

'Well there are plenty that can do that without you sinking to the depths of those that are paid to serve.'

'Oh come on now Mirabelle, don't be mean.'

'Get out! go on, get out! and take this tray with you.' Shoving the tray into her hands, she pushed Eilish on the shoulder in the direction of the open door.

For the next few days, Poppy was sent with Master Teddy's meals until he asked if Eilish still worked downstairs. Poppy blushed and said she did.. 'As much as I appreciate you bringing my food Poppy, why doesn't Eilish bring it? Is it my sister that's upset her?'

Poppy looked towards the door in case someone was listening. 'No Master Teddy. Beg pardon but I'm not sure I should tell tales, it could get me into trouble,'

Teddy leant forward con-spiritedly, 'If we whisper and I promise not to tell, will you tell me?'

He could be funny could Master Teddy and Poppy giggled

'Well, Miss Mirabelle caught you two giggling the other day and she told her Ladyship who told Mrs Green that Eilish was not allowed to bring your meals.'

'Ahhhhhhh I seeeeee.' Teddy said with his finger to his lips. 'Okay, secrets safe with me.' and he winked at her making her giggle again.

Henry-Carmichael made a point every evening of visiting is son before dinner. He was concerned not so much with Teddy's physical problems, but his mental state. So this evening Lord Fanshaw was thrilled when his son asked. 'Papa, I think I would like to join the family for dinner tonight.'

'Really! But that's wonderful. I'll send Martin up to help you dress. Are you feeling better? in yourself I mean.'

'Papa, can a I talk to you? And may I ask that our conversation stays between ourselves.'

'Of Course

And so it was agreed that Teddy would continue to study for his exams with a private tutor, and the nursery would be turned into a study.

When this was discussed with Miss Pinkerton, she seemed very relieved. Lord Fanshaw had for some time thought the time had come to dispense with the service of a Governess. Miss Pinkerton smiled delightedly. 'As a matter of fact your Lordship, I have been wondering how to broach the subject of my retirement, but I didn't want to let you and her Ladyship down. I too feel that Miss Mirabelle is no longer in need of my services, and my sister, who is recently widowed, is feeling rather lonely and wishes me to reside with her.'

'Well that's excellent news Miss Pinkerton, we certainly will be sorry to see you go, but you have served us well over the years, first with Joseph then the twins, and I'm sure it's not always been easy.'

Miss Pinkerton smiled as she thought *"That's an understatement if ever there was one"* instead she said. 'It's been a pleasure Sir and I'm sure Master Teddy will surprise us all.' She didn't add that he was the best of the bunch.

When Henry-Carmichael informed his wife of the new arrangements, she threw up her hands in horror. 'What on earth am I supposed to do with Mirabelle each day, the girl's never happy unless she's up to some mischief.....'

'I've thought of that my dear. Mirabelle needs to learn some discipline. It won't be long before she "comes out" and is presented at Court, so I think a spell at a good finishing school is called for.'

Lady Fanshaw fell back onto her cushions, relief sweeping over her. 'I couldn't agree more, but you need to be the one to tell her.'
'

CHAPTER 5

Just as Lord Fanshaw had promised, when Eamonn reached the age of twelve, he was given a position in the stables at Wynchampton.

He did so well in his first year that Eilish thought, at last, her time had come, then Eamonn dropped his bombshell.

Unbeknown to anyone, Eamonn had other plans, although he liked his job and loved working with the horses, he could see beyond that. He had his father's ambition and to this end had not only befriended the blacksmith who came to shoe Lord Fanshaw's horses, he had talked to him and eventually asked if he could be apprenticed to him.

His hopes were dashed when he was told that apprenticeships had to be paid for and could his Mother afford it? Eamonn saw his longed-for plans melting away. Undaunted to told Joe Blackstone, he would work for him for free to learn his craft. Joe thought about this offer and knowing how hard Eamonn worked at the Hall, it was an offer he couldn't refuse, so he went to see Shelagh to discuss the matter.

When Eilish heard of this she was devastated, and railed against Eamonn telling him how selfish he was being. With no money coming in, how on earth would she be able to embark on her dream!

One afternoon there was a terrible commotion when Poppy answered the bell to Lady Fanshaw's sitting room, only to find her Lady's maid and companion, Nancy Brown, collapsed on the floor and Lady Fanshaw in hysterics.

The doctor was called and Nancy was taken to hospital where she was thought to have had a stroke. Far from sympathising with the poor woman, Lucinda could only think that she would not have a Lady's maid at her disposal, and with Miss Pinkerton gone and Mirabelle leaving for Switzerland any day now, who would she have to see to her every need?

Henry-Carmichael said he would place an advert in the papers immediately but in the meantime she would have to put up with the parlour maids, after all there were three of them. But when Mrs Green was asked to send one of the girls for this duty, and asked for volunteers, none of them wanted to volunteer. 'Well come along then, one of you has to do it or shall I choose? it's a step up.' She declared 'And you might be kept on permanently as Lady's maid.' If she thought this would encourage them she was sadly mistaken. The thought of being at Lady Fanshaw's beck and call at all hours of the day and night, filled them with horror. They'd rather stay as parlour maids

'I'll go' Eilish said, raising her hand timidly

Mrs Green pursed her lips. If truth be known, Eilish would probably be the best one for the job. Over the years, despite the bumpy start, Eilish had shown herself to be a hard worker, doing whatever job she was given to perfection and with pride. But how would the mistress take having the Irish girl in the position? Hopefully, she would be too desperate to care.

Eilish was told to change into the uniform of Lady's maid and present herself to her Ladyship.

After knocking on her door, and instructed to 'Come', Eilish entered. Lady Fanshaw looked up from her magazine.

'Oh, it's you. What do you want? I didn't send for you.'

'No your Ladyship, Mrs Green sent me, I'm to act as your Lady's maid until the new person arrives

'You!' Lucinda screeched as she sat up quickly then lay back, the effort had made her breathless. 'Send Mrs Green to me, what on earth is the woman thinking about!'

Eilish ran back downstairs and found Mrs Green in conversation with cook. They stopped talking and turned as Eilish ran in. 'What now!' Cook said exasperated

'Her Ladyship wishes to speak to Mrs Green, she's not impressed having me as her Lady's maid.'

The Housekeeper shook her head, "Impressed!" where did this girl find such big words. Sighing heavily, she walked out saying, 'Follow me Eilish.' and back they went upstairs. On reaching the drawing room, she stopped. 'Wait here.' she instructed Eilish, then knocked and entered when called to do so.

'Mrs Green, Whatever possessed you to send that Irish girl to me? Are you out of your mind?' she demanded. If Mrs Green had her way, she'd give this fat lump of lard who thought she was a Lady, a piece of her mind. When Miss Pinkerton announced she was to leave and retire to live with her sister, Beryl Green wished it could be her. She'd spent more than twenty years with this old harridan, but a job's a job, so she took a deep breath and was her usual polite self.

'I am sorry your Ladyship but I thought out of all the parlour maids, Eilish would be the best seeing as how she can read and write, and as his Lordship explained, it is only temporary until a new, more suitable person can be found,'

Lucinda mulled this over. Green was right of course and it did mean the girl could write letters on her behalf and read to her when she wanted to be read too. 'Very well then, send the stupid girl in.'

Mrs Green sent Eilish back in, and returned downstairs, smiling as she went. Eilish may be Irish, but stupid she was not, she muttered to herself.

As Eilish was now permanently upstairs, it was easier for her
to pop along to Teddy's study in the afternoon when Lady Fanshaw had her rest.

A new member of servants had been installed since Teddy's talk with his father and that was one Arnold Rosebury, a retired school master, who was happy to come out of retirement to teach young Master Teddy, though that hadn't been his first thought when approached by Lord Fanshaw. Arnold had been recommended to help in Teddy's studies to get him into University. But Mr Rosebury, had taught the aristocracy in the past and knew that most of them didn't want to learn as money would get them in anywhere, and they were often impudent and lazy, so it was a nice change when he reluctantly met Teddy and found him to be like his father, polite, intelligent and a pleasure to teach.

Teddy's other request to his father was that he be allowed visits from Eilish who he found interesting to talk to and seeing that Teddy needed a young person to converse with, Lord Fanshaw agreed, though these visits would be kept low key and preferably from Mama who they knew would object.

With Joseph back at university, and Mirabelle away in Switzerland. The house settled down again and relative peace was restored.

Various Lady's presented themselves for interview with her Ladyship but were dismissed as being too fat or too thin, too ugly or too pretty, too young or too old. Fed up with advertising, Lord Fanshaw gave up and when asked why no further applicants presented themselves, Henry-Carmichael fibbed to his wife stating that no further applicants had been forthcoming.

Eilish continued in her position as "temporary" Lady's maid, though this was made all the more palatable when her quarterly pay was handed over to her and Lord Fanshaw informed her she was to receive the official wage her position commanded especially as she was now eighteen.

With her new income, Shelagh told her she must keep half and save for the time when she could apply for a position in one of the department stores in Oxford.

Several months on and Eamonn had taken up his apprenticeship with Joe Blackstone, the blacksmith, and Teddy had won his place at Oxford.

The only blot on the landscape, well two actually, was Mirabelle and her brother Joseph.

Mirabelle had been sent home from the finishing school with a none too favourable report on her conduct, but as preparations for her "coming out" were in hand, she had little time to cause mischief, unlike her brother, Joseph.

He'd finally been ejected from Oxford and no amount of money would persuade the board to change their minds. He now spent his days with his father, who was desperately trying to teach him the running of the estate, but more often than not, Joseph only succeeded in upsetting the workers. When Lord Fanshaw confided in Duncan McGregor, who was his Agent and Manager, McGregor didn't mince his words. 'If you'll allow me Sir, I think young laddie needs to learn from the bottom up. The men won't take kindly to a young whippersnapper telling them what to do when he has nay a clue of what he's talking aboot.' He declared in his no-nonsense Scottish accent. Lord Fanshaw hid his smile, there weren't many that would dare speak their mind so honestly to his Lordship, but McGregor was a tough but fair, highlander who wasn't never disrespectful.

'I think you're right, McGregor. Why don't we try it? I'll speak to Joseph and tell him of our new arrangement.' As he turned to go, he smiled ruefully at McGregor. 'Good Luck!'

And so it was that young Master Joseph was placed in the hands of Duncan McGregor, how the other workers had laughed over that. 'God help him' was amongst some of the remarks when they heard the news. 'Serves him right, Old McGregor will sort him.' And so he did.

Joseph hardly lasted one day under Duncan's direction, before the lad was running to his father.

'Father! I want him sacked!' Shouted Joseph as he stormed into his father's study without knocking that first evening.

Lord Fanshaw slowly looked up from the ledgers he was studying. 'Do you indeed. Well before we discuss this further, perhaps you could try conducting yourself like the gentleman you are supposed to be, Now please leave my office, then knock on the door and wait to be called in.'

'But Father....' he spluttered, beside himself with rage

'I said OUT!' his father roared. Joseph did as he was told, knocking and waiting to be called, still seething with rage. As soon as he heard the call, he entered. 'Now, sit down Joseph and don't interrupt me.' His fathers voice was now modulated and Joseph relaxed. 'The reason I've put you to work with Duncan McGregor, is that you know very little of the workings of the Estate or farming. If you are going to be my successor, and more importantly, make a continued success of the Estate, you need to know everything there is to know, from ploughing to sowing to harvesting of crops. You need to know about diseases of plants, nurturing, storage and selling. Then there's the livestock and your servants. Everything and everyone has to be cared for if the Estate is to progress and keep up with your competitors. There is so much to learn about being a landowner, and you must know every detail if you are to command the respect of your workers and the tenant farmers, because without them, you will have no Estate. Without their respect, which doesn't come from bullying, they will cheat you and work against you.'

Joseph listened and said nothing. He did not agree with his father's take on how to run the Estate. As far as Joseph was concerned, when he was in charge, he'd horse whip the buggers who'd dare disobey him. He'd never cow-tow, as he saw it, to the workers when he was in charge. But for now, he would keep his own council and be seen to go along with his Father's ideas. He nodded as if in agreement but swore that McGregor would be the first to go when he was in charge.

With the comings and goings of seamstresses, shoemakers, milliners and caterers, Mirabelle's Coming Out, was in full flow and Mirabelle in her element. There would be much socialising, luncheons, dinners, balls, theatre outings both at Wynchampton Hall and at other stately homes and Mirabelle was sure she would receive many invitations.

Cook was livid when one morning a toffee-nosed Frenchman invaded her kitchen announcing that he had been selected by her Ladyship, to be in charge of the kitchen on certain dates, and he
would be bringing his own entourage of servants. He would, he informed Cook, give her these dates so that the week before his arrival she would ensure the kitchen and all its equipment would be cleaned and scrubbed to within an inch of its life as he, Monsieur Da le Roué could not be expected to work in anything short of an immaculately clean kitchen. After that remark, Cook was apoplectic with rage. 'How Dare he!' she screamed, 'A man whose Countrymen eat snails and frogs legs! The cheek of it! Telling me my kitchen is dirty, I'll swing for him!'

There came another angry outburst, when Mrs Green returned from a mornings discussion about all the functions to take place at The Hall, to announce that Miss Mirabelle had to have a maid to accompany her when she visited other houses, to help dress her and arrange her hair. This dubious honour was to go to Poppy, who wailed in despair and pointed out that she had no idea how to dress hair and couldn't Eilish go instead. Mrs Green looked uncomfortable before saying that 'Miss Mirabelle and said in no uncertain terms that it was not to be.......the Irish girl.' She turned to Eilish. 'I'm sorry Eilish, I am only repeating what Miss Mirabelle said.'

Eilish smiled. 'Don't worry Mrs Green, I quite understand, and I can't say I'm sorry, though I do feel for Poppy.'

Later that afternoon, Poppy waylaid Eilish. 'What am I going to do Eilish? I haven't a clue how to dress hair?'

'Why don't you practice on me? I'll stay on after work and you can try out different styles.'

'Yes, but you don't live in Eilish, it will make it so late for you to walk home, it could be dangerous.'

'Well if you don't mind and we don't tell anyone, I could sleep with you. As long as my Mammy knows I'm staying over, she won't worry.'

'Oh, would you really do that for me?

'Of course, we're friends aren't we?'

And so for the next few weeks, Eilish would sneak upstairs to Poppy's room and lay low until Poppy joined her, then the girls would work well into the night practising hairstyles, which often left them tired and exhausted the next morning. But it paid off when one morning, Mirabelle sent for Poppy to try out some hairstyles. They had a week to go before the first ball and Mirabelle was amazed at Poppy's skill. She had been ready to have a tantrum, thinking Poppy would be useless, but was speechless when she looked in the mirror. 'Oh my goodness! Am I not beautiful? Poppy! I'm speaking to you.'

'Yes Miss, very beautiful.' She agreed but wished she could add if you weren't so fat and podgy and took more baths.

Although a bath was drawn for Mirabelle each day, it hadn't escaped the maids notice that it was rarely taken, which left a certain odour about her person.

With a week to go, The Hall was a hive of activity. The first dates were to take place in London and the surrounding Counties. Clothes and accessories were pressed and packed, the carriage which would take her and Mama was washed, polished and brushed until it gleamed. There would be a separate carriage for Poppy and the luggage but this didn't receive the same treatment. The horses also underwent plenty of grooming, everything had to be perfect. The only bit of light on the proceedings as far as Poppy could see, was the two coachman who had been chosen to drive the carriages. One of them was sweet on Poppy, and she didn't object to his attentions.

At last, early one morning the group set off. With her Ladyship and Miss Mirabelle gone for two whole weeks, the servants could relax. The only troublemaker left was Master Joseph and as he was now firmly under Duncan McGregor's wing, and exhausted from a day's work with him, he didn't have the energy to be disruptive, that was until he caught Eilish in Teddy's old nursery.

Lady Fanshaw had instructed Eilish to give a thorough clean of the nursery and to pack all books and any remaining toys away getting a footman to take them to the attic. She had decided to turn it into another sitting room, it would save her coming downstairs each day, save her legs, she said. Oh wonderful, thought Eilish, that'll help you get even fatter. Although Eilish hadn't relished spending even more time with Lady Fanshaw, she would have liked to see London and the other places they were due to visit. She'd assumed she would be expected to go with them but when nothing had been mentioned, she spoke to Mrs Green.

'Yes, that is strange.' The housekeeper said. 'Her Ladyship's said nothing to me, so I better enquire in case she automatically thinks we know. Leave it with me.'

Two days later, Mrs Green called Eilish into her sitting room and told her that her Ladyship didn't require her but would share Poppy, with Miss Mirabelle It transpired that what her Ladyship had actually said was that she didn't want anyone knowing she had an Irish girl in her employ.

So this was how Joseph found her, down on her knees packing books into a box. He'd come in looking for a ruler he told Eilish, but that was quickly forgotten when he saw her down on her knees. It had been a long time since he'd had a woman and his male frustration was beginning to get the better of him. Why not take one of these wenches, that's what they were there for. It was a given fact that all maids were fair game to the aristocracy, and they should think themselves lucky to be chosen.

'Well, well, well. And what have we got here?' Eilish turned. She hadn't heard him come in but noticed that luckily, he hadn't closed the door. If she was quick, she could probably make it out of the room and get away. The house was silent so she knew all the maids would be downstairs in the kitchen, so her cries, would not be heard from here. Standing up slowly she faced her tormentor. 'What are you doing?' he asked as he walked slowly towards her.

'I'm clearing the nursery as her Ladyship asked me too.'

'Are you now.' He said as he sat down on the edge of the desk. 'Well that must be boring, wouldn't you like to have some fun?'

'Not really.'

'Not really? Oh how impudent you sound when you say it like that. Don't you realise that one day this will all be mine, The Hall, the land, the Estate, and if you're a lucky girl, you could still be employed here, Em.... what do you think of that?' he was speaking very slowly and quietly but in a menacing way.

Eilish knew it was dangerous to rile him but couldn't help herself. 'Not a lot.' she replied to His face paled and the sniggering smile disappeared. Just as she thought she would have to make a run for it and hope she reached the door before he did, she was saved.

'Master Joseph, Master Joseph.' Daisy came hurtling up the stairs and into the nursery. 'Mr McGregor says he's found one......'
Daisy froze and took one look at Eilish and knew she was terrified. Daisy knew in an instant that she must not leave the room without her. 'And you're to come immediately! Eilish, Mrs Green says she needs you Now!' she lied

'Eilish will be down shortly. Now you can go Daisy.'

Daisy dashed forward grabbing Eilish's hand and dragging her out of the room. 'No Sir, she has to come now or I'll get into real bother so I will.' And before he could stop them, the two girls flew down the stairs.

As soon as they were through the green baize door they stopped, breathless. 'Did I do right Eilish? I made it up about Mrs Green, but you looked so frightened.'

'Oh Daisy I could kiss you. I don't know what I would have done if you'd gone and left me, Thank goodness you thought so quickly, thank you, thank you so much. From now on I'm going to lock the doors if ever I'm on my own.'

'Don't blame you. That Joseph's a nasty piece of work, I wouldn't trust 'im as far as I could throw 'im.'

Eilish did not want to go back to the nursery, so found other things to do, but the following day, she knew she had to return and finish the job she'd started. When she did return, she made sure she'd
watched as Joseph went off with Mr McGregor, then locked the nursery door once inside.

Two weeks later, their peace was shattered with the return of Lady Fanshaw and Mirabelle. Far from being excited and full of life, Mirabelle was in a foul mood, complaining about the other debutantes' and how stuck up and unfriendly they'd been and how the beaus were few and far between. Mirabelle was furious, that she'd been regularly shunned and had hardly any dance partners. Her dance card was never full and only the ugly young men approached her. One of them thought she was so desperate, he suggested they walk in the moonlight and when she did, he tried to take advantage of her. He was the son of some Duke, so her Mama marched her over to complain about his son's behaviour, whereupon the Duke looked Mirabelle up and down and retorted, 'Beggars can't be choosers!'

When the servants heard about this, they knew they shouldn't, but couldn't help laughing. It was Poppy who of course came back with all these tales and also said the entire fortnight had been a nightmare. If it wasn't Lady Fanshaw shouting at her it was Miss Mirabelle, she was glad to get back for a rest.

Lady Fanshaw tried to convince Mirabelle that when they hosted her ball, the others would soon change their attitude. Wait until they sample Monsieur Da le Roué's cuisine she told her daughter.

'Talking of Mon sewer Dale Roo or whatever he calls himself.' Cook said one morning 'We'll give the place its usual scrub down the night before he comes and if 'e don't like it, tough!

CHAPTER 6

At six A.M. on the morning of the Wynchampton Hall ball, there was a loud banging on the kitchen door. Daisy went to open it and almost fell over as the door was pushed abruptly open and in walked twelve men, all smoking foul smelling cigarettes, and stinking of garlic.

'What is the meaning of this?' Cook shouted. At once they all began babbling away in a language Cook did not know nor did she want to know. Boxes and crates were brought into the kitchen and dumped unceremoniously on her table where she had just started preparing for the Master's breakfast. "ere! You can't leave that lot on my scrubbed table, I'm preparing his Lordships breakfast!' The Frenchmen took no notice and proceeded to bring in yet more boxes and crates.

'O*u est le magasin de glacé?'*

Mrs Green and the butler had heard the commotion and came running into the kitchen. By now Cook was on the verge of tears.

Ou est le magasin de glacé!' One of the strangers shouted at cook. Cook, Mrs Green and Stanley looked at each other in bewilderment.

'WE DON'T UNDERSTAND YOU. Mr Stanley said slowly and loudly. 'SPEAK *THE ENGLISH*'

'NO ENGLEESH, Ou est le magasin de glacé! ' The little French man shouted at them again.

'I think they're asking where are the ice boxes.' A small voice piped up. Everyone turned and saw Eilish standing there.

'Oh please, don't tell me you speak French as well?' Mr Stanley said running his hands through his hair. 'For heaven sake, whatever next!'

Eilish didn't like to say that she'd picked up some French when sitting with Master Teddy when he had his lessons with Mr Rosebury, because his Lordship had asked Teddy to keep their meetings a secret.

38

'Well you can deal with them then.' Stanley said storming out.
Cook and Mrs Green looked at Eilish, appealing for help. Faltering, she manage to convey to the French team that she would show them where the Ice boxes were kept but they must remove all their boxes and crates immediately so Cook could get on cooking his Lordships breakfast. Eventually, with some broken and mispronounced French plus lots of hand gestures, arm waving and finger pointing, Eilish got everything under control.

After the maids had taken breakfast up for his Lordship and Master Joseph, Cook made a start on the trays for Lady Fanshaw and Miss Mirabelle, which were taken up by Eilish and Poppy. Just in time for "Mon sewer Dale Roo," as Cook insisted on calling him, arrived. Swaggering in and followed by the earlier entourage. He rudely told cook and all the others, to go, all except Daisy, who he announced was to stay behind in order to wash up and clear up. Daisy looked terrified until Cook Shouted, 'No! Clear up yourself!' and grabbing Daisy by the arm, bustled her out with the rest of Wynchamptons domestic servants, who all trooped along to Mrs Greens sitting room.

Poor Mrs Green was at a loss for words and went to seek guidance from Mr Stanley, who when he heard they'd wanted to keep Daisy, said Mrs Green should send Eilish back to help.

Mrs Green thought this very unfair but had to obey. When Poppy was sent to dress her Ladyship, Lucinda was furious that Eilish had been sent to skivvy for the French, and sent Poppy back with a message to Mrs Green, to send Eilish immediately to her, and to tell that little Frenchman she was paying him enough and he was not having her servants, not any of them!

Mrs Green duly visited the kitchen and before she could speak was horrified at the state of Cooks domain. Cook would have gone mad if she'd seen this. Instead, she called Eilish over and sent her to her Ladyship, passing on Lady Fanshaw's message to Monsieur De la Roué in no uncertain terms, and leaving him no time to ague as she left hurriedly.

The noise coming from the kitchen as De la Roué and his team prepared the evenings banquet, was incredible. There was banging of pots and lots of shouting, that none of them could understand as it was all in French, and the below-stairs servants were glad they were well out of it.

As the guests arrived, they were shown to their rooms, footman and maids were running upstairs and downstairs as orders were issued hither and thither. Some of the young ladies had bought their own maids. And of course, all had their Mothers as chaperones.

Those daughters and wives of Dukes and Barons, looked sniffily around at Wynchampton Hall, whilst others, less wealthy than the Fanshaw's, looked on in wonder.

Poppy was called to dress and arrange the hair of Mirabelle, who informed her that after her "Coming Out", she was to tell Mama, that she wished too now have her own Lady's Maid, and she'd chosen Poppy. 'What do you think of that!' She beamed at Poppy, who stared back at her in horror. Far from the honour that Mirabelle thought she was bestowing on Poppy, it was actually Poppy's worst nightmare. 'Aaah, I can see you're so overwhelmed with gratitude, you're speechless!' Mirabelle declared. Poppy just nodded dumbly, over my dead body! Poppy thought.

In Lady Fanshaw's room, Eilish was dressing her Ladyship. 'You won't believe the poor efforts we were offered at the various dinners, I couldn't begin to use the word "Banquet", we were subjected too. When I told the Duchess Balthorpe we'd hired a French chef and his team, she looked furious, and when Baroness Wellington, having been told by the Duchess, asked me if this was correct, she remarked, "Oh dear, I do hope you will not be disappointed, the Baron and I always find French cuisine rather unpalatable." Of course, I realised this remark had been made out of pure jealousy, so I replied, "It depends on the skill of the chef you can afford to employ!" She laughed. 'I can tell you, she didn't like that one bit, oh no.'

As the evening got off, the servants enjoyed peeking through the green baize door, as the ladies made their way to the ballroom where a Master of Ceremonies, especially employed for the evening, announced the guests.

Lord and Lady Fanshaw, Mirabelle, Joseph and Teddy, who'd returned from Oxford just for this evening's ball, stood in line welcoming their guests.

As the dancing struck up, and the young ladies dance cards were filled, Mirabelle was thrilled that her card, for the first time, was full. It did not occur to her that this was because it was her ball, and to not have danced with her would have been extremely bad manners. It did not however, come to her attention, that none of the young gentleman attending, had booked more than one dance!

The visiting Lady's maids were allowed to sit up in the gallery overlooking the ballroom in case they were needed, so the servants of Wynchampton also took advantage of this. It was because of this that Eilish witnessed. Not once but several times, cruel snubs to Teddy when he asked, one by one, to place his name on their dance cards. Although Teddy walked with the aid of leg irons, he no longer used his crutches, only a stick when he was particularly tired.

Eilish watched as he gallantly lumbered around the room, and at each snub, she felt hot tears of anguish prick her eyes. How could they not see beyond his disability. This was one of the kindest, sweetest young men you could ever wish to meet, and as it had been some months since she'd seen him, Eilish realised with a jolt, what a handsome man he had become. What she would have given to have been able to run down into the ballroom and danced the night away with Master Teddy. Master Joseph on the other hand, had the young ladies positively fighting for his attention. Eilish shuddered when she recalled the narrow escape she'd had with him when he'd caught her in the nursery, and not for the first-time thanked God for Daisy's timely intervention.

Suddenly the orchestra stopped playing and dinner was announced. Each lady was escorted into the dining room, which looked spectacular.

Cut glass sparkled, Chandeliers shimmered, with gold edged bone china and cutlery gleaming on the snow-white damask tablecloths. All this having been overseen by Mrs Green and Mr Stanley.

Down the centre of the table were six silver vases, each three-foot tall, holding huge floral displays which reached another two feet. This, Eilish thought, was rather over doing it as it had the effect of completely obliterating the person sitting opposite.

The menu had been written in French and although some of the guests were familiar with this, some were not and it seemed to cause some confusion and annoyance.

When the menu was translated, there were a few looks of distaste. Teddy was amused and a little embarrassed at his mother's pretentiousness but his mother was not, Papa appeared oblivious.

First came the Oysters sat on beds of ice on enormous silver platters with quarters of lemon . The gentleman tucked into these with gusto but only a few of the ladies partook. There followed large trays langoustine, accompanied by small bowls of tepid water to rinse one's fingers after shelling, then platters of frogs-legs, which really caused quite a commotion. Again, the gentlemen did not appear bothered and tucked in.

Bowls of what was said on the menu to be soup came next but was extremely unpalatable as it was so thin it resembled lightly flavoured brown dish water with slices of onion and what appeared to be small squares of toasted bread.

Bowls of mixed green salad appeared next much to those not aware of the French way of dining. This course was just to clear the palette. The fish course followed which was greeted with sighs of relief, this was more like it, though there was a strange sauce with it.

The meat course followed and to everyone's delight appeared to be beef, much later, they were to discover it was in fact horse meat. This was accompanied by a sliced potato dish, swimming in cream and strongly tasting of garlic, not everyone's choice. The vegetables were indescribable, so anyone's guess.

Those who had struggled with the menu so far, now looked forward to dessert, they were disappointed, because, as the French do, out came the cheese first. Thankfully, at last, dessert then coffee. The gentlemen adjourned to the drawing room, to take Port and cigars, the ladies to the sitting room for liquors and chocolates and the young people back to the ballroom for more dancing and extra fun now that parents were otherwise engaged.

The guests maids returned to sit quietly in the background to await their Mistresses to ready them for bed. Teddy wandered up to the gallery to watch the dancing, which is where Eilish found him.

Eilish had gone back to tidy the gallery and put the chairs away. 'Master Teddy? Why aren't you downstairs?' Teddy turned and smiled at her

'Are we back to "Master Teddy" again, I thought we were Teddy and Eilish.' Eilish laughed.

'Ah but that was in the privacy of the nursery when you were studying, now you're university student, a young man of the world, going places I shouldn't wonder.' she teased

'Oh Eilish, it's so good to be back here talking with you.'

'Well you should be down there enjoying yourself with all the other young things.'

A sad look spread over his face as he looked down on the dancing couples below. 'Ah, but you see, there is one problem, I can't dance.'

'Nonsense, you can walk can't you?'

'Sort of.' He said ruefully. 'But no one wants to dance with me.'

'Then they don't know what they're missing! I'd dance with you if I were down there, in fact, I'd dance with no other!' She said acting petulantly, which caused them both to have a giggling fit.

Teddy wiped his tears of laughter. 'Oh Eilish, you really are a tonic. Right, Miss Eilish, will you do me the honour and have this dance with me?' Teddy bowed and Eilish getting into the spirit of the game, curtsied and replied, 'Why Sir you do me a great honour.' and he took her in his arms and together they stumbled round the gallery to the music. When the music came to an end, Teddy did not release her and Eilish realised she did not want him too. His arms were surprisingly strong as he held her and she knew she did not want to let him go but knew she should. It was as if a magnet was holding them together. Eilish looked up and he was looking down at her. It seemed that neither could pull apart. They heard someone coming and reluctantly let each other go. Just in time, Eilish continued to stack the chairs as Joseph appeared. 'Well, well, well, and what goes on here? Is my little brother trying to have a little fun with the Irish?'

'Don't be so disgusting!' Teddy said, 'We're not all like you!'

'Well no, I suppose those things on your legs do rather hamper you. But I could always give you hand, help you on so to speak, know what I mean?'

'How dare you speak so disgustingly! Teddy raged

Joseph laughed, 'What are you getting so uptight about, it's only Irish.'

'And don't call her that, her name's Eilish!' Teddy was roaring at him. Neither had noticed the music had stopped and their row was being witnessed from below. 'I think it's time you went back downstairs.' Teddy hissed. When they turned round Eilish had gone. Teddy felt awful and vowed to see her before he went back to University the following day and apologise for his brother's despicable behaviour.

Joseph on the other hand was furious. He'd seen the pair dancing up in the gallery, which was why he'd gone up there. He'd also seen them when the dance had ended and how they'd stayed together, their arms about each other and he was consumed with jealousy. By the time he reached the gallery, the music had started up again but Eilish was now busy with the chairs but it didn't fool him, he knew what he'd seen. How on earth could she be like that with that cripple, but reject him, Joseph. He vowed he would get even, she would pay for her behaviour.

According to her Ladyship and Miss Mirabelle, the ball had been a great success. But when the downstairs servants entered the kitchen after the French team had left, they were appalled, in fact Cook burst into tears. The state of the place was as if there'd been an explosion. Monsieur De La Roué had turned his nose up at Cooks equipment saying he would bring his own, however, he'd obviously decided to use hers after all, and every pot, pan, dish and plate had been left in a filthy state.

Every knife, spoon, fork and ladle had been thrown into the sink, on top of which was thrown roasting pans thick with congealed fat. Every surface included the long wooden table, which was always scrubbed white, was stained and burnt where hot pans had been placed. The servants looked on in horror, and although they were all dead on their feet, none had the heart to turn away and leave her and the two scullery maids to get on with clearing up. Everyone rolled up their sleeves and set too. It was gone one A.M. before the last guests left, and those staying, went to their beds. Then they had to attack the ballroom and dining room. Mrs Green said the rest could be left until the morning as it was now after three, and she doubted very much that any of the household or their guests would be down that early for breakfast. She thanked Eilish for staying on to help, who had agreed with Poppy, she would share a bed with her for what was left of the night. They had less than three hours before getting up and starting again.

Mrs Green was correct about the early rising, except for Lord Fanshaw and half a dozen of the male guests who'd opted to go for an early morning ride, none of the maids were called to their mistresses till much later.

All the guests were leaving promptly after breakfast, but to their dismay, and Lord Fanshaw's embarrassment, neither his wife or daughter put in an appearance to thank them for coming or wish them a safe journey home. It didn't take long for word to circulate to those families who hadn't attended, at the disgraceful way they'd been treated, and the awful dinner they'd been subjected too. None of this bothered Lady Fanshaw when she got to hear of the gossip, putting it down to jealousy. And when Mirabelle's dance card was once again empty at the next ball, she vowed and declared she would attend no more functions, with the exception of her daughter's presentation to the Queen, at the famous "Queen Charlotte Ball", which was always held at London's Grosvenor House.

The Queen Charlotte Ball was the highlight of the debutante's coming out. They all wore gowns of pure white, supposed to symbolise purity, and would enter the ballroom by descending down the grand staircase. It was a truly magnificent sight, after which, many a young girl would be beaming, having landed herself a future husband during the season. If he had a title that was good. If he had money, that was even better, but if he had both title and money, then that was excellent. Love? Well that didn't come into it, but if it did then you had won the jackpot, though that was rare. Many a young bride lived to regret saying yes, but then many a groom lived to regret asking the question!

As Lady Fanshaw had to accept her daughters lack of popularity, it was decided to go to London on the eve of the ball, leaving early in the morning having reserved a room at the Grosvenor, in which to change. Poppy was duly summoned to accompany them, only on this occasion she had to travel with them so had no respite from the grumbling pair.

At last it was all over and everyone breathed a sigh of relief, including his Lordship, who'd had enough of the general disruption, and the constant demand on his finances. He was also bitterly disappointed that Mirabelle had not attracted a suitable marriage partner, or even a possible beau.

And finally there was Joseph, who had been reported to him, by his Agent/Manager, as bone idle, unreliable and, *'If he were my wee laddie, he'd 'ave a swift kick out in ta the real world!'*

Typical of Duncan, he didn't mince his words. Lord Fanshaw shook his head in despair, something would have to be done.

CHAPTER 7

Life settled back to normality, though Mrs Green had cause to point out to her Ladyship, that since she'd taken Eilish as her Lady's maid, which she understood was only to be temporary, and now Miss Mirabelle had taken Poppy as her personal maid, Mrs Green was short servants. She would need at least two more parlour maids if she was to continue the high standards of efficiency to the running of The Hall as her Ladyship required. Lady Fanshaw said she would speak to her husband about engaging more servants, but when she did, Henry-Carmichael was not impressed. He was still reeling from the cost of his daughter's "Coming out" and as Mirabelle seemed to laze about most days and Lucinda appeared to " rest" her entire day, he found it hard to believe that after attending to their needs on rising and retiring, there was any reason that both maids could not return to their duties below stairs. Servants issues restored, those below stairs, were happy.

One afternoon, Mrs Green informed Eilish, that her Ladyship, wished her to go through her wardrobe, checking her gowns for cleaning and mending, then to give the room a thorough spring clean.

Eilish was pleased to see that her Ladyship was downstairs and would therefore not be interfering as she worked.

As it was a hot summers day, Eilish opened the windows to let in some fresh air, something the room hadn't had for years, she suspected. She was enjoying herself sorting the gowns, petticoats and under garments, most of which smelt strongly of her Ladyships body odour and would need cleaning. Taking them all downstairs, she informed the other maids she would join them later and returned to her Ladyships room. This was noted by Mirabelle, who was bored and looking to create mischief.

Eilish had just started to wipe out the wardrobes, when she heard the door open quietly and turned to see who'd come in. Seeing it was Mirabelle she turned back to her work and continued wiping out.

Suddenly she felt a kick on her bottom, the force of which propelled her face forward into the wardrobe, as she was on her knees. Regaining her balance, she stood up and confronted her attacker. 'What did you do that for?' Eilish demanded, knowing she was probably out of order speaking to the daughter of the house thus, but Eilish didn't care.

Mirabelle was aghast. 'How dare you speak to me in that tone you Irish bog girl!' she screamed, red with rage, her fat chins wobbling. There was no reply to this as Eilish knew, she'd never get the better of her tormentor. Shaking her head in disgust, she turned to continue her work, but Mirabelle was not leaving it at that. 'What are you doing in Mama's room? And where are all Mama's gowns? Are you stealing them? You are aren't you?'

Turning slowly, she was about to reply, when the door opened and in walked Joseph. The words she was about to speak froze on her tongue. She remembered the last time he'd caught her in a room, but at least on this occasion, they were not alone, Miss Mirabelle was here, he could do nothing while she was in the room. But Eilish hadn't bargained for the depth of depravity or the loathing Mirabelle had for the Irish girl, nor had she any idea of Master Joseph's lust and revenge he had for her.

'Well, well, well. We meet again Irish. I wondered what all the noise was about. Have you been upsetting my little Sister?'

'Yes, she has brother, she's been rude and arrogant, and I only asked her what she was doing in Mama's boudoir.'

'I see. Me thinks Irish is much too spirited and like any filly, she should be tamed, what say you sister, would you like to see this young filly tamed?'

'I most certainly would brother. What have you in mind?'

Joseph slowly rubbed at his crotch in a certain grotesque way which made Eilish's blood run cold. She looked towards the door but Joseph was standing in front of it and unlike last time, he'd closed it on entering. Now he turned and slowly turned the key in the lock.

Squealing in excited delight, Mirabelle clapped her hands. 'What have you in mind brother?'

'I'll show you little sister what happens to naughty girls who don't know their place.' Joseph walked slowly towards her and Eilish backed away. Suddenly she felt the backs of her legs make a connection with the side of the bed. She was trapped, she could not move forwards, backwards or sideways. Fear gripped her, surely, he would not attack her in front of his sister. But Mirabelle appeared to be enjoying the situation, encouraging her brother. Surely, she would realise his intention and demand he stop in the realms of decency, but Eilish was not to be so lucky.

Suddenly, Joseph lunged forward pushing her onto the bed and pining her arms above her head. 'Hold her arms down sister! And don't let go.'

Eilish cried out as she felt Mirabelle's weight climb onto the bed behind her and take over her arms from Joseph. Eilish continued to struggle, begging him to stop, until Mirabelle hit her so hard across her face, it made her head spin.

'You see sister how she quietens down, signs she is obviously enjoying it.'

'Does she have any draws on? 'Mirabelle screamed in excitement, spittle running from her mouth onto Eilish's hair and forehead.

'Calm down sister, and I'll tell you.' Joseph said as he roughly fumbled under Eilish's skirts, tugging at her underwear. Far from enjoying his attack, Eilish had closed her eyes to shut out the sight of his evil, lavishes face, and her humiliation. 'This filly is easily tamed, a bit too easily for my liking, a bit more sport would have been more fun.' He declared

'Stop calling her a filly.' Mirabelle demanded. 'Fillies are nice creatures, she's nothing but a dirty Irish bog slut.'

As Eilish lay still, unable to fight a fight she knew she could not win, Joseph ripped at her underclothes and yelped with excited delight. As he undid the buttons to his trousers, Mirabelle screamed with lustful excitement. 'Take her brother, take the slut down.' And she clapped and bounced about the bed like a hoyden.

Eilish, her arms now free, tried to lift them but the blood inside them had drained and left her weak and unable to move. Suddenly she felt a searing pain between her legs as Joseph tried again and again to enter her. Finally he plunged inside crying out in lustful joy as tears of shame ran down Eilish's face.

Mirabelle joined in the degradation, shouting obscenities as her brother destroyed an innocent young girl.

Eventually her ordeal was over and Joseph rolled off her, sweat dripping off him. 'There sister.' he said panting. 'What sport, and guess what? Surprisingly she was a virgin, I've always wondered what it would be like to deflower a virgin, and now I know, it was thrilling.'

As brother and sister enjoyed their action, Eilish grabbed her chance of escape. Pulling herself of the bed, she stumbled towards the door unlocking it and racing down the stairs, through the green baize door and out of the kitchen, much to the shocked surprise of the servants working in the kitchen who stared after her. Mrs Green had been talking to Cook, both looked up and stopped when they heard the door crash open and hurried steps running down into and out of the kitchen. Parlour maids, scullery maids and one of the footman stared after the fleeing girl, her long red hair, normally tucked into her mob cap, now in disarray. Her clothes were torn and was that blood on the hem of her petticoat? Mrs Green ran out after Eilish but by the time she reached the yard, the girl was long gone.

Everyone stared as the housekeeper returned, hoping for some explanation. They wouldn't have long to wait.

Eilish did not stop running until she reached home, bursting into the cottage and collapsing into her mother's arms.

Shelagh had been ironing when her daughter flew through the door as if all the devils in hell were after her. Catching her in her arms, she realised she'd been attacked, but how, why or when, she would have to wait until the sobbing, hysterical girl felt safe enough to relay her ordeal.

After some time, Eilish became calmer. Shelagh patted her daughter's shoulder and she winced. Looking at her, Shelagh saw under the grubby tear-stained face, bruises starting to appear. She felt a seething anger against whoever did this to her dear, sweet child. 'I'll make you some tea, then if you can, I want you to tell me everything.' Eilish nodded and he mother stood to make the tea into which she stirred, three spoons of sugar.

As Eilish sobbed out her ordeal and the names of her attackers, Shelagh felt such a rush of rage, had the perpetrators been stood in front of her, she was sure she'd have killed them, beaten them with her bare hands. When Eilish finished her story, she looked pitifully up at her mother. 'Mammy, please don't send me back there.'

'Don't worry me darlin' you'll not be going back to that hell hole, and those who have done this will pay!'

'No Mammy Please No! I'm so ashamed!'

'Tis not your shame, darlin, tis theirs, and I'll see they never get the chance to do this again, even if I have to go to the Garda.' Shelagh had returned to her Irish roots, her language, and her native tongue. 'First I'll get you a bath and then you are to go to bed and rest.'

Shelagh bought in the tin bath and placed it in front of the fire. Despite the warmth of the day, Eilish was shivering from shock. Filling the bath with warm water, Shelagh added handfuls of dried herbs she knew would help to sooth her daughter's bruised body. She was shocked as she undressed Eilish and saw the dried blood and what looked to her like semen, She closed her eyes and prayed that her daughter would not be with child.

Later, with Eilish now warm and resting in her bed, Eamonn arrived home surprised to see his mother emptying the tin bath, and it not Saturday, the day they usually bathed. As he opened his mouth to speak, Shelagh held up a hand to her son.

Eamonn, Your dinner is on the stove, Eilish is in bed, she's not well so please do not disturb her. I have to go out but I won't be long.'

Eamonn frowned 'What's.......'

'Please son, don't ask me questions. Your sister is not well and it's of a personal nature. Now, I must be off, I won't be long, have your dinner.' Wrapping a light shawl about her, Shelagh McGovern was on a mission, every bit as dangerous as a wild tigress protecting its cub.

Marching up to Wynchampton Hall, she was aware Lord and Lady Fanshaw would be at luncheon with the family. So much the better, she wouldn't have to wait to get them all together. In her bag, she carried her daughters stained and torn petticoats. What she had in mind to do she knew was probably in poor taste but she didn't care, what those two deviants had done to her daughter deserved everything they got and Lord Fanshaw could do for her daughter now, what he'd once promised, speak on her behalf to one of the owners of an Oxford department store.

As she headed for the front entrance of Wynchampton Hall, she was prepared for the butler who would try and refuse her entrance, telling her to go round to the servants entrance, but she would have none of that. She was going in the front entrance and nothing would stop her.

Pulling the bell rope several times, she waited, ready to pounce and push her way in as soon as the heavy oak door opened. As she waited, she began to shake, whether through fear or rage she could not decide, Suddenly the door opened and Harold Stanley stood there and immediately started telling her to go to the servants entrance. He neither knew nor cared who she was or what she wanted, he just knew by looking at her clothes that she should not be coming to the front of The Hall. Shelagh didn't wait, instead, pushed past him. Taking him with such surprise, he couldn't stop her and she was half-way down the large entrance hall before he could get to her.

Not knowing which way it was to the dining room, Shelagh faltered, giving Stanley time to catch up with her. Grabbing at her arm, he tried to stop her from going further. Shelagh rounded on him and as best she could, addressed him in her most cultured of English voice she could muster.

'Unhand me you oaf! And take me to your Master, I wish, No! Demand to speak to his Lordship.'

'How dare you, you, you....

'If you're struggling to know my name, I'll help you, it's Mrs McGovern, Eilish McGovern's Mammy, Mother.' She corrected herself. Stanley still had hold of her arm and was hurting her such was his grip. 'Unhand me this minute!.' At that moment, a door behind them opened and a voice Shelagh recognised said.

'What on earth is going on?' And seeing who it was, turned angrily to his butler. 'Stanley! Just what do you think you are doing? Let go of Mrs McGovern this instant. My dear. I'm so sorry, please, come to my study, you are obviously upset, whatever is it?'

'I'm sorry M' Lord but this woman....'

'Enough Stanley, you can leave this to me. Please return to your duties.'

Shelagh took a deep breath and quietly composed herself. 'I beg your pardon your Lordship for bursting in on you like this, but what has befallen my daughter this day, and in your house.......' She got no further before bursting into tears of despair.

'My dear Mrs McGovern, Please, come with me and tell me what on earth has happened to Eilish.' Recalling the accident that had killed this poor woman's husband, Henry-Carmichael feared for what he was about to hear, nobody had mentioned any accident since he'd returned home. 'Sit.' he said gently pressing her into an armchair. 'Would you like some tea, a brandy perhaps?'

Shelagh shook her head, dabbing at the tears with her handkerchief, and apologising at the same time.

'Now tell me, what has happened in my house that I am not aware of?'

Shelagh told him how her daughter had returned home that afternoon and the ordeal she'd suffered and by whom. Haltingly, she removed the torn and stained clothes from her bag. Lord Fanshaw stared silently and tight lipped at the clothing.

'I should inform you that my daughter will not be returning to work here, and that when she is feeling better, I would ask you if you would be kind enough, as you promised some years ago, to speak to your contacts at any of the Oxford department stores, for any opportunity suitable for Eilish,'

Lord Fanshaw slowly nodded. Then looking up he said.

'My dear Mrs McGovern, I cannot tell you how distressed I feel that Eilish should have suffered so at the hands of members of my own family, it is unforgivable and I can assure you, both will be punished. Of course, I will look into your request and I'm sure, we will be able to find a suitable position. She is an intelligent, hardworking young woman and I know, has gained the respect of her colleagues. Now, is there anything else I can do to help or ease her distress?'

'No Sir. But I would like to thank you for your kindness and understanding.'

'Not at all.' As he stood, the interview over, Shelagh stuffed the torn clothing back into her bag. 'May I have those?' he indicated her bag. 'I will return them.' Shelagh was unsure but handed them over. 'Thank you. I will show you out.'

After he'd closed the door behind her, Lord Fanshaw stood for several minutes trying to calm himself, clenching and unclenching his fits and grinding his teeth. As he stood there, Harold Stanley reappeared, trying to ingratiate himself with his Lordship but before he could open his mouth, Lord Fanshaw barked at him. 'Not now! Stanley' and marched into the dining room, thrusting open the door and slamming it behind him.

Lucinda, Mirabelle and Joseph, who had been laughing heartily at something, jumped and turned to look at Henry-Carmichael. He leaned against the door and when Joseph realised his father was glaring at him, he was frightened. Never before had he seen such rage in him and Joseph knew real fear.

Slowly, Henry-Carmichael withdrew the torn, blooded and semen-stained petticoats of Eilish. He held them in the air and was rewarded as his son's face flushed red, then paled and his daughter gasped in horror and noticed the fear on her face.

'I see you recognise these .' He growled

Lucinda looked from one to the other. 'What is going on? And why did you leave the table?' she admonished her husband.

'Perhaps you would like to tell your Mama, how these clothes came to look like this and to whom they belong? He spoke quietly and calmly, but his words came out menacingly as he glared at his son. Joseph stared back at his father, terrified, swallowing nervously. 'No?.... Mirabelle?... What have you to say? I understand you took part. Want to tell your Mama?' He roared and both his children jumped in terror.

'Really!' Lucinda said 'What on earth are you getting yourself into such a rage over some little peasants rags..... 'she got no further.

'Silence!' he roared. It was now Lucinda's turn to jump, she rarely heard her husband speak to her like that even though she knew she'd exasperated him over the years. 'If you'd been a better Mother, spoilt them less, and not allowed them to run riot because you were too lazy to pay attention to them, perhaps they wouldn't have turned out to be the most useless, unpalatable couple of people to walk on Gods earth. Get up! He roared as he lunged forward, grabbing his son by the throat and dragging him from his chair, and bodily throwing him across the room where he landed, winded, up against the door, shaking with fear.

Lucinda screamed, Mirabelle cried and ran to her mother fearing she would be next, and Stanley ran into the room only to be screamed at to, 'GET OUT!'

The beating Joseph took that evening would never be talked about or forgotten by anyone. Fearing he might kill the boy, Harold Stanley ran for Duncan McGregor, the only man he knew who would be able to deal with his Lordship. Duncan ran into the room and caught his Lordships fist as he was about to land yet another punch. Pulling his Lordship firmly but gently out of the room, he helped him to his study ordering the butler to bring the brandy bottle, glasses and send for a doctor for the boy.

By the time he'd calmed himself, his Lordships sobbed his disappointment that his eldest son and only daughter could behave like gutter snipes. But as far as he was concerned, Joseph had deserved his beating and his daughter's punishment though not violent, would be severe and would come.

Duncan called Mrs Green and Poppy to assist her Ladyship and Mirabelle to their rooms, and the doctor when he arrived, asked Duncan to assist him in getting the boy to his room, where he treated him, stating that he had several broken ribs, bruising and lacerations, but he would live, and knowing Josephs reputation thought, had he been disciplined as a child, this beating would not have been necessary.

When Duncan later, joined his Lordship again in his study, they both drank another brandy together and Henry-Carmichael, thanked him for his intervention.

Having told Duncan of Joseph and Mirabelle's attack on poor defenceless Eilish, he told him that he was disinheriting Joseph from the Estate and on his death, the title and Estate would go solely to Teddy. On the morrow, he would be contacting an old army contact he had, and Joseph would be joining up, not as an officer but starting at the very bottom of the ladder and would only receive promotion if he earned it and not from privilege.

As for Mirabelle, he knew of a convent whose Nuns worked with the poor, in London. He was sending her to them.

As Harold Stanley listened at the connecting door of the library to his Lordships study, he now knew what all the commotion had been about, and was quick to tell Mrs Green, in "strictest confidence" he said "Of course" she said who went straight to tell Cook, "In strictest confidence " she said "Of course" said Cook, who straight away told.....and so on.

The following day Lord Fanshaw made immediate contact with the owners of three stores he was acquainted with. The first, a haberdashery, run by two sisters Ellen and Sissy Andrews, the second a small linen shop run by a Mrs Doris Wright who had big plans to extend her business to include ladies fashions and furniture, and finally the largest of them all that sold ladies fashions, shoes and other accessories. On other floors, bedding, general linen, rugs, kitchen ware, china glassware etcetera. All said they would be happy to interview the young woman, on Lord Fanshaw's recommendation and if suitable, they would be happy to employ her,

Without further ado, his Lordship paid a visit to the McGovern's cottage. Shelagh, welcomed him, surprised to see him so soon after her appearance at The Hall. After asking how Eilish was and apologising for the dreadful abuse she'd suffered, he told her, that when she was ready, he had three stores that were happy to give her an interview with regard to employment and training. They were also able to offer accommodation. He handed over the of names, addresses and details of the stores. Eilish took the papers from him, thanking him for his kindness, shyly trying to hide her face which was badly bruised and swollen.

The following day Henry-Carmichael sent a telegram, to Brigadier Sir James Halliwell, an officer he'd briefly made the acquaintance of several months previously. He invited him to Wynchampton Hall for a long weekend, as there was something of a serious nature he wished to discuss with him

Next he wrote a letter, but this would be sent by courier as it was also a matter of urgency

Meanwhile he had ordered Miss Mirabelle to be confined to her room and her meals to be taken there. Poppy, other than taking her meals to her, was to serve the young girl in no other way. This came as a surprise but relief to Poppy.

Similar was ordered regarding Master Joseph, but as he was still recovering from the severe beating he'd received from his father, that wasn't too surprising. His meals were to consist of soft food, porridge, broths, and stewed fruit as this was all he was able to eat at present.

Lord Fanshaw visited his children each day, to make sure they were behaving themselves and to let them know there would be substantial changes to their lives over the next few weeks, of which he would enlighten them in due course. Both Mirabelle and Joseph were nervous of the fate that awaited them.

Lady Fanshaw said nothing about the fact that neither of her children appeared at table on the first evening after the trouble. She was angry and sickened at the way Henry-Carmichael had attacked darling Joseph but scared to death of saying anything. In all her years, she'd never seen such violent rage, nor had she forgiven him for the way he'd spoken to her, and all because of that little Irish peasant, leading her son on, then running to her "Mammy", disgusting word, and complaining!

But when three days later they still hadn't appeared, she decided to speak to him and find out what was going on. She was shocked at his response and the callous way he addressed her.

'You mean to say you have not visited either of your children to see how they are?' He asked her scathingly

'Well no. Your attack on, on p.......' She was about to say, poor Joseph, but changed her mind when she saw the sharp way he looked at her. '....our son, left me quite traumatised, and my heart has suffered quite severely.'

'Who says?'

'Sorry?'

'You said, your heart has suffered severely, I asked you, who said? Have you seen the doctor?'

'Well no......'

'Well how do you know your heart has suffered severely? You talk rubbish Madam. You need to get some fresh air instead of laying around all day feeding yourself with endless sweetmeats, get some exercise.' He turned to go. 'Oh, and by the way, we will have company over the coming weekend. Brigadier Sir James Halliwell, he will arrive Friday sometime in the afternoon and leave mid-morning Monday. Please inform Mrs Green and Cook.' Henry-Carmichael walked out leaving Lucinda speechless and wondering, What Now?

Entering his study, he rang for Harold Stanley. When the knock came on his door, he bade him enter. Since the trouble, Harold had been keeping out of his Lordship's way as much as possible, fearful of doing something that might antagonise him.

'You rang your Lordship?'

'Yes Stanley, we have a guest arriving on Friday, mid-afternoon, he will stay until Monday. He is Brigadier Sir James Halliwell, please designate one of the footman to look after him during his stay. That is all.'

'Yes your Lordship.'

After her husband had left her, Lucinda rang for Mrs Green, informing her of their impending guest and telling her to make ready a room and inform Cook that her Ladyship would be sending down menus to cover the days their guest would be staying.

Speculation was rife below stairs as they all tried to think who and why this army officer was coming. 'Do you think they're going to marry Miss Mirabelle off to him?' they giggled, but when he arrived, they realised that he was old enough to be her grandfather, let alone her father.

To Mirabelle's surprise she was told she was to bath and dress each day of the Brigadier's stay, and to present herself at the table at every meal, and to conduct herself in the way she'd been brought up. Poppy was once again told to attend Miss Mirabelle, who was now very subdued.

On Friday afternoon, a carriage rumbled up to the entrance of Wynchampton Hall. The butler opened the door, and Martin, the delegated footman, stood ready to take the Brigadier's portmanteau to his room, unpack for him and press his dinner jacket should it be necessary.

On hearing of his arrival, Lord Fanshaw made haste to welcome Sir James.

Impressed with Wynchampton Hall, after coffee, his Lordship took the Brigadier on a guided tour. Sir James was intrigued to know why he'd been invited and with such speed. After a pleasant luncheon, where they'd been joined by the Fanshaw's rather overweight daughter, who the Brigadier had found, a rather sulky and unpleasant young woman, his Lordship took him into his study. Over brandy and cigars, Henry-

Carmichael, made his request. He wanted his son to enter the army, but unlike most of the aristocracy, he wanted the young man to start at the very bottom and only promoted when he'd earned the right to do so.

Lord Fanshaw then went on to explain, that Master Joseph had flunked his exams to get into Oxford university, so his father had "bought" him in, thinking that three years of study might make him grow up. Five years later, having not achieved a pass in any exam, Oxford threw him out. More
time spent working on the Estate with his father's estate manager had shown no improvement. The young man had continued to cause a catastrophe that could still have dire results, only time would tell. Either way, Joseph lacked discipline, respect and purpose. Henry-Carmichael could see no other way.

Brigadier Halliwell clasped his hands together and leaned forward resting his elbow on Henry-Carmichael's desk. He had a broad smile. 'My dear Sir, you've come to the right person. Many a young scallywag has found himself in the Army and discovered he's met his match. Give him to me and in three years' time, you won't recognise him.'

'I was thinking more like ten years.'

'Up to you Sir, up to you. We can sign him up for ten years, it can be arranged, and after telling me what you have, I think it would be ideal.'
Lord Fanshaw sighed with relief. 'When do you want him?' He asked. The Brigadier twiddled his moustache thoughtfully.

'Why don't you introduce us?'

Upstairs, Joseph was idly flicking through magazines and trying to plot revenge against Eilish, Teddy and his father. The door to his bedroom opened and in walked his father with a man in uniform.

'Joseph, I would like to introduce you to Brigadier Sir James Halliwell, Sir James, my son Joseph Fanshaw.'

'Good afternoon young man.'
Joseph could only look at this old man with the silly handlebar moustache and sneer. He rudely nodded, insolently acknowledging the Brigadier, which infuriated his father, but excited the Brigadier. The more insolent they were, the more he enjoyed bringing them down to earth. The Brigadier nodded, a slow smile creeping across his lips, though Joseph was taken aback at the steely gaze in the man's eyes. The

smile didn't reach the man's eyes. Joseph realised he might just have made an enemy.

On Sunday, Joseph was informed he was to get up and join his father and his guest in his study.

Whilst they talked, a list, written by the Brigadier of what items of clothing and personnel effects should be packed, had been handed over to Mr Stanley and together with Martin, the footman, Josephs things were hurriedly packed into a trunk, ready for his Journey to the barracks the following morning, where he would begin his training.

When Joseph first heard of the plans made for him, he was filled with horror, but thinking about it, his father had obviously planned this as a short sharp shock but he, Joseph, would cause such commotion, they'd be kicking him out and he'd be back at Wynchampton in a matter of weeks if not days. Yes, this could be quite a lark.

It would be less than a week when Joseph discovered his mistake and found he'd been signed up for ten years and the penalty for escape would be a court martial and prison.

CHAPTER 8

When Lucinda discovered what had befallen her son, she flew into a rage, hobbling on a stick, so bad was her walking, that she almost fell on reaching the library were her husband was thumbing through a book.

'What is the meaning of this ?' She screeched. 'My son, your heir, and you send him into the army! He could be killed do you not realise this? And what would happen then? Who would run the Estate?'

Lord Fanshaw looked up and stared at her for a few moments. What had happened to the young woman he'd married all those long years ago. True, he'd learned too late from his father, that she'd been the bane of her parents, but to him, she'd come over as sweet and quiet, how wrong could you be. A small smile escaped from his lips, it didn't go unnoticed by his wife. 'What are you laughing at?' She screamed at him. Henry-Carmichael cringed at the sound of her course voice.

'If you would stop screaming at me like some fishwife, I will tell you.' But Lucinda was not in the mood to wait, and he'd called her a fishwife! Lifting her stick, she lunged at him then stumbled. She was lucky her husband caught her before she fell to the ground but easing her into a chair, he stepped back abruptly. 'That is not the only change to be made in this house. I intend to send Mirabelle to a Convent, where she will work alongside the nuns, helping the poor.'

'You're going to do what!' Lucinda opened her mouth to say more but the words never came. Suddenly, she pulled a strange face, her hand went to her heart and her face became contorted. Her mouth slackened and she started to dribble profusely. Now it was Lord Fanshaw's turn to be worried. This was no act. Pulling urgently on the bell cord, he summoned help.

Later that evening, he had cause to reflect. He felt guilty for what had happened, but then reminded himself that Lucinda had brought this whole scenario on herself.

The doctor had assured him, it was a stroke waiting to happen. He told Henry-Carmichael that he'd been on at Lady Fanshaw for years about her weight and lifestyle, but she'd threatened to bar him if he didn't mind his own business. The tempers and rages which he said were of her own making, and her lack of self-control, only exacerbated her condition. He, Lord Fanshaw, was not to blame. But Henry-Carmichael was not the only one to blame himself. When Mirabelle found out her Mama was now lying in bed with a stroke, she flew for her father.

Three weeks later Lucinda Fanshaw passed away having gone into a coma, from which she never recovered.

The funeral was not a big affair as Lucinda had not been popular amongst the Fanshaw's acquaintances.

Joseph was given compassionate leave, though Henry-Carmichael was pleased to see he'd come with an escort, the Army wasn't taking any chances.

Teddy was also given leave from his studies at Oxford, and his father was so proud of his youngest son, as he was growing into such strong minded, determined young man, despite his
disability.

The house went into mourning, and under the circumstances, Lord Fanshaw decided that Mirabelle would remain at home, for the duration of her mourning.

Slowly the Hall returned to normal, and except for the odd tantrum from Mirabelle, life was relatively peaceful.

Despite being told many times that what had happened to Lucinda had not been his fault, Henry-Carmichael still felt he should have been more strict with his late wife and his children from the start. Perhaps then Joseph and Mirabelle would have turned out better behaved young people. He could only hope the Army could achieve something with Joseph, but Mirabelle, that was a conundrum, what was he going to do with her?

He'd received an encouraging reply to his letter to the Convent, but under the circumstances, the Convent agreed she should remain at home for the foreseeable future. Then one day he found himself outside the cottage of the woman who'd been increasingly on his mind.

Henry-Carmichael had gone for a walk, on the pretext of clearing his head. As he neared the McGovern's cottage, he slowed, then urged himself to walk past. He had never been one to look down on those commonly regarded as the "lower classes" because he saw it ,without them, there would be no workers and he and his family and others in his position, would not have any servants. And, as his servants had always served him well, he would argue, that was a particularly good reason to look after them and treat them with respect, an attitude that had rewarded him over the years, with loyalty.

But where Shelagh McGovern was concerned, he had to admit, he had other reasons for his visit here today. Over the years, since he'd come to know her, every time he'd visited her, and there had been many occasions, his enjoyment of her company had, if he was honest, turned towards affection.

He admired and respected her the way she'd conducted herself on the death of her husband, and the way she'd gone on to educate and encourage her children to better themselves, and it was Eilish that was giving him the excuse to call today.

Several weeks previously, he'd left information of three possible employment opportunities for her, and he was wondering if she'd taken steps in their direction.

Although still in mourning, he felt an urge to visit Shelagh, as he liked to think of her, though he was careful to always address her formerly. Sometimes, especially of late, since the passing of his wife, he'd also teased himself with thoughts of holding her in his arms. Giving himself a mental shake, he knocked on the door.

It was Winter again, and he rubbed his gloved hands together as it was cold. Shelagh opened the door just enough to see who it was not wanting the warmth of the room to escape, but on seeing who it was, she flung open the door with pleasure.

'Lord Fanshaw! What a surprise, come on in you must be frozen.' The pleasure with which he'd been welcomed, spurred him on to think that he was not the only one to view their budding friendship with affection. He was tempted to kiss her on the cheek, but withheld, instead, he took her hands in his and squeezed them gently. 'Sit yourself down and warm yourself. Can I get you some tea?'

'I would love some tea, and to sit in front of your fire to warm myself before I return, would be most welcome.'

Shelagh busied herself making tea and cutting slices of the seed cake she'd made earlier, whilst offering her condolences on the loss of his wife and chatting about the weather.

Lord Fanshaw smiled his thanks for her condolence, then agreed with her about the weather. He then asked after Eamonn and Eilish.

Eamonn, Shelagh reported, was doing fine. He loved working with the Blacksmith, and Joe Blackstone had informed her the boy was doing well. Eilish, she told him, had started work two
weeks previously at Mrs Wrights emporium and had been taken to the warehouses to learn about buying. Shelagh was most enthusiastic and he could hear the excitement in her voice, which made him laugh. Shelagh looked surprised, why was he laughing. 'Oh Shelagh, you all sound so happy........I'm sorry, do you mind if I call you Shelagh? I feel we have known each other for so long........and sadly, through some sad times, so to see and hear you so happy, makes me happy and my heart sing.' Shelagh's heart was thudding in her chest. She blushed furiously and busied herself putting more logs on the fire in an effort to compose herself. Without looking at him, she replied to his question with regard to him calling her, "Shelagh".

'No, of course not, as you say, a lot of water has passed under the bridge. And it's thanks to you that both my children have been given the opportunities they have.'

As he'd finished his tea and cake, he got up to go, not wishing to outstay his welcome. 'Well, thank you for your company and the refreshment. Please give my regards to young Eamonn and tell Eilish how pleased I am that she is settled in her new employment, I'm sure she will make a great success of it.' He gave a little bow and went to the door. As Shelagh opened it, he hesitated. 'May I, may I call on you again? I have so enjoyed our chat, The Hall is noticeably quiet these days.'

Shelagh smiled back at him. 'Of course you can Sir.'

'Aaah, if I'm allowed to address you as Shelagh, and as none of you are in my employ, then I must insist we dispense with Sir or Lord. My name's Henry.' He omitted the "Carmichael" it was too much of a mouthful.

His return to the Hall was made with a spring in his step, not unnoticed by his servants when they encountered him.

Shelagh thought about what Henry had said about how quiet it was up at The Hall and felt sad. She knew what he meant, as since starting work in Oxford at Mrs Wrights, Eilish had been living in, it being too far for her to walk each day, especially in the winter. And when the snows came it would be impossible. Also, Shelagh had thought, Eilish needed to get away from the sight of Wynchampton Hall.

Although the bruises and scratches Eilish had sustained during the attack had healed, they had still to await the signs of her female cycle appearing, and the following day Shelagh was relieved to receive a letter in the post from Eilish telling her Mammy, all was well. Shelagh could have cried with joy, at last, life could go on with no further fear. There was only one concern Shelagh felt for her daughter, and it was that the attack might frighten the poor girl from a future marriage. But only time would tell. In the meantime they must put it behind them and look forward with hope.

In Oxford, Eilish was gaining in confidence every day. When she'd arrived at Mrs Wrights store after being offered employment, Doris Wright began to wonder if she'd done the right thing. Eilish was like a little frightened mouse, and Doris feared that without more confidence, she'd never make a sales assistant. However, after talking through her plans for expansion, and taking her to visit the different warehouses, Doris saw an interest grow in the young girls demeanour and when she started to ask, timidly at first, questions about products, Doris knew she had the makings of a particularly good shop assistant.

Knowing where she lived, and Lord Fanshaw's request the girl would need accommodation, Doris had made up a bedroom which also doubled as a sitting room, should she want privacy.

But as Doris's husband was often away on business sourcing new stock, she was often lonely in the evenings and longed to talk about her plans for the emporium's future. This she was able to do when shortly after Eilish moved in, Doris told her she was always welcome in her sitting room. Most evenings Eilish would join her, eager to learn more and more about the business. It was on one of these evenings that Doris made the suggestion to Eilish that she may like to train as a buyer.

Skelton Wright, Doris' husband, was in China dealing with a Chinese maker of beautifully, coloured, silk rugs. Eilish had never seen anything like these before but was excited when Doris showed her a sample. The empty shop next door was to be renovated, as soon as the purchase was completed, and the walls knocked down so customers could walk from one department to another.

At the moment, Doris' store consisted of ladies fashions, underwear and shoes on the ground floor, gentlemen's out fitters on the first, and on the second, was the large apartment where the Wrights and now Eilish, lived.

Eilish was excited when she listened to Mrs Wright as she addressed her, talking about her dreams for the store. Eilish felt a trickle of excitement, sure that here was a future for her as well.

Eilish returned home each Saturday after the Store closed, and as the weather got colder, Doris insisted Eilish take a carriage which she, Doris paid for.

Shelagh and Eamonn looked forward to Eilish coming home, and although Eilish was well fed at Doris' she nevertheless looked forward to her Mammy's home cooking.

Because Eamonn was still working for free as Joe Blackstone's apprentice, and since the demise of Lady Fanshaw meant there was no more work for her, Eilish insisted on handing over her wages to Shelagh. Unbeknown to Eilish, her Mammy put away a few coppers each week in a jar for Eilish's future, as Shelagh had been requested to take in other sewing from acquaintances of the deceased Lady Fanshaw.

Soon, Christmas would be upon them, so Shelagh decided the time had come to make lists of preparations, food and presents to be bought and made. She'd just sat down one snowy after-noon when there was a knock at the door. Opening it, she saw, much to her delight, Henry standing there, covered in snow. 'Come in, come in, whatever possessed you to come out in such weather?'

He laughed as he pulled off his boots, banging the clumps of snow from them, then took off his coat. Taking these items from him, Shelagh took them to the kitchen telling him to warm himself by the fire. 'So, what brings you here today of all days?' she asked on her return.

'Well, I was thinking about Christmas and discussing with Cook, then I thought of you, and I had an idea. I was going to send you a turkey, but thought, why not ask you, Eilish and Eamonn to join us up at The Hall for Christmas Day? Teddy will be home and I..........What's wrong? You look terrified, what have I said?' Henry looked shattered as he stared at Shelagh who equally looked horrified. Realising that her reaction had upset him, she pulled herself together.

'Oh Henry, that is so thoughtful, but surely you must realise that it would be impossible.'

'Why?' He looked puzzled.

'But Henry, don't you see.......we couldn't possibly come to The Hall, can you imagine the servants' shock at having to serve us? I mean, whatever would Cook say when she knew who she was cooking for, and your butler...' Fleetingly, Shelagh thought back to the last time she'd seen the butler, when she'd barged in like a mad woman after Eilish had been attacked. She shuddered at the memory. 'And your housekeeper.' she finished meekly.

Henry sat back his elation dashed. Ahead of him all he saw was a lonely Christmas. True, Teddy would be home, that at least was some comfort to look forward too. He sighed deeply, and of course there was Mirabelle. Whatever made him think Shelagh and Eilish would want to sit down at the table with his daughter after what had happened. When would his loneliness ever end. Shelagh had been too kind not to mention the attack, instead, she used the servants as her excuse.

He shook his head. 'I honestly do not think I should need the permission of my servants whom I entertain, but as you say, it would make you feel uncomfortable, and I would never want that. Would you at least accept a turkey as a gift for me?' He asked, almost pleading. Shelagh smiled and leaning forward patted his hand. 'Just a small one, or I won't be able to get it in the range. Now, how about a cup of tea and some of my fruit loaf?'

'Oh, you temptress.' Henry said feigning shock and laughing.

Shelagh asked how Teddy was getting on, and Henry told her proudly that yet again, he'd passed his latest exams with flying colours. He also told her about his bafflement on what to do with Mirabelle.

As he was leaving, Shelagh had an idea. 'I don't suppose.....look I....well the thing is... Oh I'll just say it and if you think it a bad idea I won't be offended. I can't invite you all to dinner on Christmas day, there's just not enough room, but if you and Teddy, and of course Mirabelle, would care to come for tea, I'm sure we could make room.'

Henry's face lit up. 'I think it's a wonderful idea and yes, I'd like to accept and I'm sure Teddy would love to see Eilish again.' He would ask Mirabelle, but was sure she'd be horrified at the idea, so he said nothing to Shelagh. They parted, wishing each other a Happy Christmas and said, 'Until Christmas day.'

Eilish arrived home on Christmas Eve loaded with presents from Doris and the other servants working in the store, and for her Mammy and Eamonn.

Shelagh had been baking and cooking for days and had decorated the cottage, complete with a small tree Eamonn had brought home.

It was almost midnight before they went to bed as they had so much to talk about and were excited about Christmas Day.

Shelagh was up at six A.M. to get the fires going and the range ready for the turkey and was soon joined by her daughter. Mother and daughter set too, preparing vegetables and putting the pudding on to boil. When Eamonn eventually arrived downstairs, there was just time for a quick bowl of porridge before they set of for church.

Up at The Hall, Christmas day was a quite different affair. Their Christmas day's service was held in the chapel in the grounds of Wynchampton Hall. All the servants attended as well as Lord Fanshaw, Teddy and a sulky Mirabelle The vicar who conducted the service was the same who took the service in the village, though The Hall's service was held one hour later. Looking around him, Lord Fanshaw wondered in future if it wouldn't be better for him and any servants who wanted too, to go to the village church.

Service over, they returned to the Hall where his Lordship gave out the quarterly wages, along with a gift for each of the servants. Normally these would have been chosen and purchased by his wife, now deceased, so he'd asked Mrs Green to do the honours, wrap and label them.

Next, he, Teddy and Mirabelle exchanged gifts, though from Mirabelle, neither he nor Teddy received anything, her excuse being she hadn't felt like making the journey into Oxford.

Dinner would have been a miserable occasion, had it not been for Teddy, who chatted nonstop, such was his enthusiasm for his studies and his time at the University, where despite his disability, he was making friends.

As they were finishing dessert, Henry announced that they had been invited out to tea that afternoon. When he told them by whom and where, Mirabelle was horrified, well that didn't surprise him, but Teddy was thrilled.

'How is Eilish Father?' he asked 'I've often thought about her.'

Mirabelle made a snorting noise of derision, which her Papa ignored. 'She's very well, she's...... well I'll let her tell you all about it.'

They left the Hall just after four and set out to walk to the village. After thanking the servants for an excellent meal, his Lordship said not to wait up for them, and to enjoy the rest of their Christmas Day. The servants did not need to be told twice and soon pushed the table back to give room for dancing. It wasn't long before music could be heard as one of the grooms struck up with his fiddle, another with a mouth organ and another with a concertina. They clapped and cheered and Cook and Mrs Green later brought out a supper of hams, cold turkey, cheeses, bread and what was left of the plum pudding.

Ale was brought out, port-wine, and a fruit punch for the young ones, and the girls. Mrs Green, Cook and Mr Stanley took the opportunity to have a sherry, which after a glass or two, soon had them giggly.

It was almost midnight when their fun was brought to a halt. Mirabelle, furious that everyone but herself were enjoying themselves and angry that her papa and Teddy had gone to that "peasant house!" as she called it and was in no mood to allow the servants to enjoy themselves no matter what her father had told them.

Storming through the green baize door, she stamped down the stairs and screamed at them above the music to 'Stop this racket now! My Papa will hear about this and you will be lucky if you are not all looking for employment after this disgraceful show of debauchery!'

They all looked at each other stunned, for hadn't his Lordship said they were no longer required this day and to enjoy themselves. Quietly, they thought it prudent, to clear up and get to bed.

At the McGovern cottage, Teddy and Henry-Carmichael, had, had the most enjoyable afternoon and evening. Both Teddy and Eilish were surprised at how familiar their parents were with one another, using each other's Christian names quite casually. Eilish was shocked and looked uncertainly at Eamonn, who didn't appear to notice as he was engrossed in the small train set, Lord Fanshaw had given him. When she looked at Teddy for his reaction, she saw he had a little smile on his lisps and amused, merely winked at her.

Lord Fanshaw, as Eilish still thought of him, gave both Eilish and her Mammy, a set each of beautifully, lace edged, embroidered handkerchiefs, for which they thanked him profusely, and for the turkey. Eilish's eyes opened wide when she saw her Mammy hand over two gifts to Teddy and his father of a cigar each. She started to wonder what had been happening between them when she was away Monday to Saturday and made a mental note of speaking to Eamonn when their guests had gone.

They'd played a card games with great hilarity, as Eilish proved to be hopeless, then came a game of skittles, which was difficult because there wasn't much room, and last, Shelagh encouraged Eilish to sing some Irish ballads, and Teddy entertained them with tales of the happenings at University, and mimicked some of the students and tutors, which had them in stitches.

Eilish helped her Mammy lay out a mouth-watering buffet, with a fruit punch to wash it down, and Henry presented them with a bottle of sparkling wine, which they used to toast each other, and to thank Shelagh for a beautiful spread.

When the church clock struck midnight, Henry and Teddy, took their leave, after thanking them all, once again, for a wonderful time.

It had stopped snowing as father and son walked home, tired but happy and laughing. It was a clear bright moonlit night and the stars twinkled in the dark, midnight blue sky. As Henry-Carmichael stared up into the heavens, there was a sadness that overwhelmed him, why was there such a gulf between the so-called classes. They were all human beings, made of the same flesh and blood, did you not both bleed when cut? And in his opinion, if everyone had the opportunity for education.... look at Shelagh and her children. He shook his head in sad bewilderment.

Teddy had also been deep in thought and wondered if it would be possible to mention what had been on his mind, and after seeing how friendly his Father and Eilish's Mother appeared, now might be a good time.

'Father, I wonder, would you have any objection if I wrote to Eilish while I was at University.'

'What about?' He asked, puzzled

'Oh, just to keep in touch. She was telling me all about her work. It's wonderful to think that she is actually being trained as a buyer, I thought that was a Male dominated area, but Mrs Wright seems to be a very forward-thinking lady. She says that women can do anything that men can do.' Both men were silent while they thought and digested Mrs Wrights, thinking. 'I'm not sure that I can believe that completely.'

'Nor I son. I can't imagine a lady working down a coal pit, or firing hot iron in a blacksmiths can you? but it's good to know Eilish is finding it interesting and enjoying it.'

'She said it was all down to you and she'll never be able to thank you enough.'

Lord Fanshaw smiled. 'It was little enough.' He replied.

'So, what do you think?'

'Mm?'

'Writing to Eilish?'

His father stopped and pondered the question. 'You do realise that one day you will take over from me.' He started to walk again.

'But Father......Joseph, one day he will return when he has done his stint in the Army.' His Father's face took on a hard look which even in the moonlight, Teddy recognised as grim determination.

'Your brother is to make a long-term career in the Army, and I cannot trust him to run the Estate as I would wish. There is bad blood in the boy, and I have to protect my tenants and those who work for me now and in the future, sad to say, I'm afraid I do not have faith or trust in him.' He stopped and placing a hand on Teddy's shoulder, he said 'So I have made legal arrangements, that it should be you who inherits The Wynchampton Hall Estate. So in matters of matrimony, you should think carefully, you must choose wisely with your head, a woman who is able to be of help to you, and not a drain on your emotions, or your purse strings.'

Teddy thought about this. Did his Father think he had romantic thoughts regarding Eilish, he hadn't thought of her like that, but if he did, would it be so outrageous, so impossible? And if so what was his father's relationship with Eilish's Mother?

When they reached home, all was quiet. 'Would you like a nightcap son?'

'Thank you Father, but the walk has made my leg irons chafe my legs, so if you will excuse me, I think I will go up. But thank you, I've had a wonderful Christmas, and if I can help you with Estate matters while I'm at home, I be delighted.'

Henry-Carmichael, hugged his son, said goodnight, and took himself off to his library to enjoy a tot of whiskey.

Next morning, just when Henry-Carmichael was enjoying his morning coffee and hoping that the New Year, just days away, would bring a new peace, his hopes were dashed. He was unprepared for an angry Mirabelle, storming into the breakfast room and demanding her Papa sack all the servants after their behaviour the previous evening. He knew that the problem of Mirabelle could no longer be ignored. The girl had to be taught a lesson in civility and humility, and there was no time like the present.

'Mirabelle, help yourself to breakfast, then come and sit down, we need to talk.'

'But, but.' She spluttered.

'No buts Mirabelle, do as I ask.'

'But Papa!.'

'I said, have some breakfast. What I have to tell you is far more important and concerns you directly.

Mirabelle stood staring at her father, she didn't like his quiet tone, it usually spelt trouble. Slowly she turned to the sideboard and helped herself to a mound of food, returning to the table, and seating herself.

'Are you really going to eat all that?' Her father asked.

'Yes, why?'

Her father shook his head. 'There are some families where your plate of food would feed them for a week.' He told her.

Mirabelle shrugged and tucked in. He'd let her eat, for once she'd heard his plan, she'd probably not eat another thing for the rest of the day.

Eventually, Mirabelle placed her knife and fork down and reached for the coffee pot to refill her cup. 'Well, you said you had something of importance to tell me'

'I was planning to do this before your Mama, passed away, but when that happened...'

'Yes, and we all know who's fault that was!' Mirabelle interrupted him rudely then stopped, though not in time for her Father to reconsider his plans, in fact it only made him strengthen his resolve.

As I was saying, when you rudely interrupted, please don't interrupt again. Because of your behaviour, in the past and the present, I feel it is time you did something useful, you need to know how lucky and privileged you are. You need to see the wider world as it really is, and to that end, you will be going to spend some time in a Convent in London.

When she heard the word Convent, Mirabelle froze, but then when Papa added the word London, she relaxed. She rather liked the idea of London, and surely living in a Convent wouldn't be all that bad. She had contacts in the City, she'd soon get in touch with them and have some fun. It did not occur to her, that she may not be welcome in any of their homes, so with a self-satisfactory smile, she said nothing.

'The Convent is called "Sisters of Mercy" and they work in the community in the East End.'

'Doing what?' Mirabelle asked, not that she was really interested. It wouldn't concern her.

'All sorts. Some of the Sisters nurse the poor and sick, some help by teaching children. They also help the poor by trying to educate them in keeping their homes clean, and their children fed.'

Mirabelle wrinkled her nose. 'Why should any of that be of interest to me?' She asked sulkily.

'Because you will join the nuns in their work.'

Mirabelle's eye widened. 'I will not!'

'Yes you will. For once in your life, you will become useful, do some good in your life.'

'I'll run away! '

PART TWO

Mirabelle

March 1856

CHAPTER 9

Because of her threat to run away, Mirabelle's father kept her locked in her room for her own safety, and until arrangements could be made for her departure. Her meals were brought to her and even an attempt to bribe Poppy to leave the door unlocked, was refused. She shouted, pleaded and begged but her father stood his ground.

Eventually, Poppy came to her room one morning, with clothes she did not recognise. 'What's this? She asked picking up the white flannel liberty bodice, draws and plain cotton petticoat. The cotton of the petticoat was not the fine cotton she was used too, instead it was of a course material.

'They're the clothes his Lordship, instructed me to bring you and to tell you to get dressed. And there's these.' Poppy held up the heavy grey woollen dress with long sleeves and hardly any fullness to the skirt. The last items Poppy lay on the bed were a pair of thick black woollen stockings, a shawl and a black cape.

'Master said not to be too long, the carriage is waiting to take you to the railway station. I'm to accompany you to Oxford and hand you over to the Sisters who will take you on the train to London.' Poppy informed her, thanking the Lord she didn't have to go on one of those new steam belching monsters.

'I won't go! I refuse to dress in these peasant garments.' Mirabelle said, folding her arms and throwing herself down on her bed. Poppy was exasperated. What was she supposed to do, Mirabelle was twice the size of her, and there was no way she was going to risk manhandling her, knowing she, Poppy, would come off the worst. She didn't dare go to his Lordship so instead, went to Mrs Green, who went to the butler, who went to his Lordship.

'You have two choices.' He informed his daughter. 'You either allow Poppy to help you dress, or you can travel in your night attire covered by your cape! Your choice.' At which point he turned and went back downstairs to where Mrs Green awaited him. 'Please send Poppy to Miss Mirabelle's to help her dress, or she can travel in her night attire.' He said returning to his study.

Poppy, having received her instructions, returned to Mirabelle's room with some trepidation. When she got there, Mirabelle was sitting on her bed on which the clothes were scattered. Poppy heaved a sigh and began picking them up and offering them up to Mirabelle. Much to her relief, Mirabelle allowed her to help her dress.

When later, a very subdued and sad Mirabelle walked down the stairs, Poppy had to admit, she felt quite sorry for the young girl. Despite knowing she'd brought this all on herself with her bad behaviour, it seemed all the fight had gone out of her. As to whether that was a good thing or bad, only time would tell.

As soon as she was ready, Poppy escorted her charge downstairs to the entrance hall where Mirabelle's father awaited her. Taking his daughter firmly, but gently by the shoulders, Lord Fanshaw, looked directly into her eyes. Poppy noticed the look of great sadness he bestowed on his daughter, only for it to be returned with a look of loathing. 'I do this for your own good.' He told her. 'Now please, go, and use the time to reflect, to become a better, kinder person, and appreciate what you were born into.'

As he bent to kiss her on the cheek, Mirabelle swung away from him and stalked out to the waiting carriage. Lord Fanshaw stood gazing out after his daughters retreating back and shaking his head sadly. He turned to speak to Poppy. 'Make sure you hand her over safely to Sisters Mary Madeline and Bernadette. They will be waiting at the station for you.'

'Yes Sir.'

With no luggage, Mirabelle and Poppy settled into the carriage, and the two coachmen ordered their horses to, 'walk-on.'

Throughout the long Journey to the train station to meet up with the Nuns, Mirabelle was silent, much to Poppy's relief, though she did wonder if she was planning to make a run for it. Every time, the carriage had to slow, especially when they arrived in Oxfords busy roads, Poppy's heart was in her mouth. Thankfully, she had no need to worry, Mirabelle's thoughts of escape were planned for when she arrived in London.

As their carriage pulled in front of the station and they alighted, two Nuns in their black and white habits appeared. At first their appearance seemed frightening to Poppy, but as they came towards them, their faces lit with beaming, caring smiles, and Poppy relaxed. Mirabelle she noticed, just scowled though this apparently went unnoticed by the Nuns who greeted the young women warmly. 'My dears, how lovely to meet you, now which of you is Mirabelle?' one asked which incensed Mirabelle, and almost sent Poppy into fits of giggles that Miss Mirabelle was indistinguishable from a parlour maid!

'I am.' She said haughtily 'And it's MISS Mirabelle when you address me in future.'

The two Sisters looked at each other in surprise and smiled.

'Well, well, my dear.' Then turning to Poppy. ' So you must be Poppy,' They said shaking Poppy's hand and ignoring Mirabelle. 'Well thank you so much for accompanying this young lady, we do hope you have a safe journey back and be sure to tell his Lordship his daughter is in safe hands and Mother Superior will be in touch. Come along now Mirabelle, we must get aboard our train.' With one either side of her, Mirabelle was marched swiftly towards the platform. Poppy wasn't hanging about, she too went smartly out of the station and jumped aboard the carriage which would carry her back to The Hall.

The train journey was long and arduous, and Mirabelle began to wonder if they would ever get there. Her first sight of the smoke belching monster had terrified her and she'd instinctively shied away, only to be gripped more firmly by the Sisters and propelled forward. On board, the wooden seats were hard and the back rests were of no comfort whatsoever. Mirabelle had resolved not to speak to the Nuns however hard they tried to engage her in conversation, so she was disappointed when after what seemed like hours, neither of the Sisters had even tried to engage with her in, though they chatted away to each other like a couple of twittering birds, which only served to irritate Mirabelle even more.

As she gazed out of the window, the countryside drifting past soon mesmerised her and she dozed off into a deep sleep, only to be quietly wakened by Sister Bernadette, gently shaking her and softly calling her name.

Startled, Mirabelle jumped. 'It's all right my dear.' Sister said. 'We are just coming into the station.'

'Are we there yet, at the Convent?' Mirabelle asked

'Not quite.' Sister Mary-Madeline said rather brusquely. She wasn't usually quick tempered, but she was cold and tired, and after the way Mirabelle had spoken to them on meeting, she was not amused. She knew their charge to be difficult, Mother Superior had warned them, but she still had not expected her to be quite so rude, quite so soon.

Alighting from the train, they headed towards the exit, confident that there was no further need to hang on to Mirabelle who was looking around her, terrified. Gone was the beautiful countryside, the quiet and fresh smells of clean air and clear skies, instead, everywhere was grey with black smoke seeming to come from the sky. From the platform, she could see the roof tops of buildings crammed together with no gaps in between. There were some adults dressed like she was used to seeing them, but around her ran young boys offering to carry luggage or to find you a carriage, but it all seemed so dirty, and the noise, it was indescribable. People were shouting, train doors were slamming, and shrill whistles blew as if they were screaming in your head. She had to run to keep up with the Sisters terrified that she might lose them in this mayhem.

Outside the station they stopped abruptly and Mirabelle almost collided into the back of the Nuns.

'Why have we stopped?' Mirabelle asked

'We are looking for Tom?'

'Who is Tom?'

'The lad who is taking us to the Convent.'

Mirabelle looked around her. If she thought the inside of the station was dirty and noisy, outside was ten times worse, if that was possible. 'When I came to London for my 'coming out', it wasn't anything like this.' She ventured.

'And where in London did you stay then?' Asked Sister Mary-Madeline, knowing full well the answer to her question

'In Mayfair.' Came the answer, which was greeted with a sarcastic laugh.

'Well this is not Mayfair, welcome to London, where the other half live, and work, if they're lucky.' She added as an after thought.

'Well I can see that!' Mirabelle retorted 'Does my Papa know where you are taking me?'

'Of course

'And does he know it's like this?'

'Of course.'

'But it's Filthy!'

'Like I said, welcome to London, the real London. By the time you return home, you will be able to appreciate the privileged background you were born into, and hopefully appreciate what you have and where you live, and that it will have made you into a more compassionate young woman. We hope!'

'Well I can tell you now, I'm not staying!'

'Oh? And just.......'But Sister Mary-Madeline got no further as Sister Bernadette interrupted. 'Look Sister, look, there's Tom!' The Sisters both waved, as the wooden, horse drawn cart drew up and a scruffy lad jumped down, greeting the Sisters with a warm, cheery smile. Mirabelle groaned. Could this nightmare really get any worse?

The Nuns appeared not to notice the dirty, blackened face and hands of the lad, as he held out his hands to help them up onto the cart. As he reached out for Mirabelle's hand, she recoiled.

'Don't touch me!' She shrieked and backed away.

Unabashed, Tom grinned 'Suit yerself, get up on yer own then.' And he proceeded to climb back onto the cart and pick up the horses reigns . 'Well, you comin' or not, I aint got all night.'

Ignoring him, Mirabelle turned to glare at the Sisters who sat patiently waiting. 'I refuse to travel in that.....thing!'

'Fine, then you may walk behind, but I warn you, it's quite a distance.'

'I'll get a carriage.'

'Fine, have you the fare?'

Mirabelle was speechless. Fuming, she tried to climb into the cart, which she did eventually, but made a very unladylike exhibition of herself.

It was growing dark as Tom guided the cart through the streets of the East End of London. It became gloomier, scarier and smellier the deeper into the East End they went. Whilst the other three chatted away to each other, as though they had not a care in the world, Mirabelle looked from the cart as they travelled the roads, and what she saw horrified her. Children ran about with no shoes on their feet, though you could hardly see them, they were so dirty. They were clothed in what could only be described as rags. They passed Inns where children hung about outside, some begging from passers-by, others getting a clip round the head if they got in the way. She witnessed a piece of bread being thrown from a passing carriage and saw a mangy dog and a child, fight over it, the child snatching from the animal's mouth and stuffing it into theirs.

At one time she almost burst into tears, though they would not have been tears of sadness of what was around her, only tears of frustration and humiliation and despair, that she was here in this dreadful place. Surely her Papa would not have known to where he was sending her.

Eventually the cart stopped and Tom jumped down. 'There yer are Ladies, all safe a tickety boo.' He held out his hands and helped the two Sisters down, who thanked him. Then looking at Mirabelle he grinned up at her, cheekily. 'Well Miss, you gettin' down or ain't yer, like I says before, I ain't got all night.'

Mirabelle looked to the Nuns for assistance, but they were halfway up a set of stone steps and pulling on a bell rope. 'Excuse me!' She called after them. Sister Mary-Madeline turned and beckoned her. 'Come along Mirabelle, Tom has to go home, jump down dear, I'm sure you're young and agile enough to do that.'

Gathering her skirts, Mirabelle tottered unsteadily towards the edge of the cart and slid off the end. As she did so, she felt a sharp pain, just below her buttock. 'Ow!' she cried out. 'Something stabbed me.'

Tom couldn't help laughing. 'Ah, sorry abart that Miss, probably got a splin'er in yer bum, Nuns will see ta it. Night Miss.'

Tom climbed back onto the cart, and geed the horse to giddy-up, Mirabelle looked around her. It was almost pitch black except for the occasional streetlamp that gave off a very weak light. The whole area seemed oppressive, and unlike the places they'd come through, now there was an eerie silence. Turning to see where the Nuns were, the large oak door was opening and a small light was being held by someone, though she couldn't see properly from where she stood. Sister Bernadette turned and called her. 'Mirabelle, come along in, it's getting cold.' And it was. Gathering her cape about her, Mirabelle went slowly up the steep flight of steps, panting and out of breath.

When she reached the top, Sisters Bernadette and Mary-Madeline, were already inside.

'Hello, you must be Mirabelle. I'm Sister Gabriel, come along in, you must be hungry after your long journey?' Mirabelle was about to point out that she should be addressed as Miss Mirabelle but closed her mouth before uttering the words as she was just too tired to care, and with the offer of food, she simply nodded in agreement and followed Sister Gabriel.

'Go and get something to eat.' Mary-Madeline told Bernadette. 'I'll go and let Mother Superior know we are back.

In her office, Mary-Madeline gave her report to Mother Superior who listened with sadness at Mirabelle's rudeness and her appalling attitude towards Tom. 'Oh, and I think she may have got a splinter in her rear, when she slid off Tom's cart.'

'Oh dear, better let Sister Angelica look at that, we don't want her having an infection or blood poisoning.'

Sister Mary-Madeline went to find Sister Angelica to pass on the message, then left, muttering under her breath, and good luck with that!

As soon as she'd finished supper, Mirabelle was taken to her room, which the Nuns called " her Cell". She was still in shock at the meal she'd been given. It was a bowl of thick vegetable soup, a chunk of rough bread, and a glass of milk. But she was so exhausted she had not the energy to argue. Shown to her Cell, she was given a nightshirt, and had pointed out to her, a chamber pot, a bowl and a jug of water. There was a small square of a strange smelling soap, a towel, brush and comb.

'Sister Angelica will be along in a minute as I understand you may have caught a splinter, and we don't want it to fester, in the meantime you should get ready for bed as we rise early in the morning for Matins.'

When Sister Angelica arrived, she had a pile of something in her arms and laid them on the bed saying. 'Two calico night gowns, one shift, one petticoat, one grey dress, two pair calico bloomers, two white aprons, and one course one, two pair of woollen stockings, one pair of boots, 6 body pads. Make sure you boil those separately when your time is on you. Now, lie on the bed face down and let me look at this splinter.'

Mirabelle closed her eyes in embarrassment but did as she was told, and when Sister Angelica removed the splinter with a needle, she let out a piecing scream. Humiliation complete, Mirabelle buried her head in the rough ticking of her pillow and wept herself to sleep.

CHAPTER 10

Mirabelle did not hear the knock on the door, and it wasn't until she received a gentle shake, then a more urgent one, that she awoke. For a moment she could not think why Poppy was trying to wake her, then realised the voice wasn't Poppy's.

'Come along Mirabelle, you'll be late for matins, now come on get up and get dressed, I've put fresh water in your jug to wash with, but you must hurry.' Sister Bernadette said, pulling back the bedclothes.

'Oh go away.' Yelled Mirabelle at the same time trying to drag back the blankets and sheet. 'It's freezing and I'm tired.'

'Well that's too bad. You have no choice in the matter. Now get up and get washed and dressed, you have ten minutes and I'm not going anywhere so hurry up.' Again the bed coverings were pulled from her but on this occasion, completely off the bed. Sister Bernadette stood with her arms folded, she meant business and Mirabelle knew it was no use fighting. Reluctantly, she rolled out of bed and poured water from the jug into the bowl. The moment she placed her flannel into the water she squealed. 'It's freezing!'

'Well what did you expect? Come along now or we'll be late.'

Because it was so cold. Mirabelle was washed and dressed in double quick time and sulkily followed the Nun out of her room and along the corridor. Just before they entered the chapel, Sister Bernadette stopped and turning said. 'And tomorrow morning, make sure you're up, washed and dressed and your bed made by the time I knock on your door.'

Mirabelle's mouth fell open. 'Make my bed?'

'Yes, that's what I said.'

'But I don't know how.'

'You don't know.......? Sister Bernadette was incredulous. But then when she thought about it, she realised and remembered where Mirabelle had come from. Sighing heavily she told her. 'Then in that case, your first lesson will be in bed making. Now come along.' Opening the chapel door, she ushered Mirabelle forward, noting they were just in time.

Mother Superior looked and raised an eyebrow indicating they were just in time. Matins had begun.

It was soon obvious that Mirabelle had attended very few church services as the girl soon became restless. As soon as it was over, all the Nuns made their way to the dining room to have breakfast, which to Mirabelle's horror, was porridge, bread, margarine and a cup of tea. Mirabelle sat staring at her bowl and looking around to see it there was anything else on offer, this was not what she called breakfast. Mother Superior watched her. 'Is there something wrong Mirabelle?'

Mirabelle was almost in tears. She was so hungry and longed for the sort of breakfast put up by Cook, which included bacon, sausage, kidneys, eggs, Kedgeree, kippers and lashings of toast and home-made Marmalade. She shook her head miserably and a tear trickled down her face. Several of the Nuns felt pity for her though they all knew why she'd been sent. Even Mother Superior felt a tinge of pity, but at the same time, pleased that already the young woman was less rebellious and hopefully, would soon learn the humility and compassion her Papa desired.

'What is it Mirabelle?' Mother asked gently. The girl sniffed and brushed away her tears with her hand.

'I don't like porridge.'

'Why don't you try it dear, it's made with milk and cream and lots of honey. Unfortunately, we are unable to afford meats and fish for breakfast, though we do occasionally have some eggs, that's if the hens are laying plenty, and that should be soon, as soon as the weather gets warmer. Now, why don't you try a little.'

Picking up her spoon, Mirabelle dipped it into the bowl and gingerly took a spoonful. All eyes were on her as she tasted the sweet creamy mixture and was pleasantly surprised. 'Well?' Mother asked

Somewhat embarrassed for having made such a fool of herself, she gave a weak little smile, whispering. 'It's nice, it's very nice.'

'Oh good.' Mother said clapping her hands in glee. 'Sister Joan, our Cook will be pleased that we've made a convert of you.' At which they all laughed and continued eating. To Mirabelle's surprise, there was much chatter. And she looked around whilst listening to the Sisters.

'I didn't think Nuns were allowed to talk.' She ventured when there was a lull in the conversations.

'Ah, we're not that sort of Order. 'Mother Superior told her. 'In fact, we encourage our Sisters to talk, especially when they are out in the Community. We want the people to know they have nothing to fear from us and that we are here to help them.'

Mirabelle frowned. 'How do you do that? What do you do?'

'Well, on a Sunday, we visit the workhouse, taking a service for those who are fit enough to attend. We also take a Sunday school for the little ones, that's usually far better attended, probably because we tell stories, and the children don't get much chance to have stories told to them. Mirabelle had heard of the Workhouses.

'But isn't it dangerous? To go into those places?'

'No dear, not really, they are just people like you and me, but poor, extremely poor. People who have been unable to find decent places to work so they can afford to pay rent on somewhere to live and enough money to buy food for their family.'

With breakfast finished, Mother Superior stood to issue her orders of work to be carried out by the Sisters. Mirabelle listened at some of the jobs issued and was pleased when her name wasn't read out, so she was surprised when Mother said. 'And Mirabelle, you will be with Sister Gabriel today in the garden, so wrap up warm as it is still very chilly outside.'

Before she could protest, Sister Bernadette interrupted. 'Excuse me Mother, Just before Mirabelle joins Sister Gabriel in the garden, might I give her lessons in bed making? It appears Mirabelle has never had to do this so her bed lays unmade.'

'Of course, I'm sorry my dear but I just took it for granted. Of course, you go with Sister Bernadette and as soon as you've mastered this task you can join Sister Gabriel in the garden. Right now everyone, God speed.' And there was much scraping of chairs and general chit-chat as the Nuns went about their chores.

Mirabelle followed Sister Bernadette back to her Cell, she wasn't sure which was worse, making her bed or garden duties.

By eleven O'clock, Mirabelle found herself out in the garden having made her bed a dozen times until it was deemed good enough for Sister Bernadette. She had been given a rather musty smelling coat to put on as Sister told her she would not want to be getting her cape dirty. She was only slightly relieved when Sister Gabriel told her that today, they would be working in the greenhouse, planting seeds that would later go out into the garden. Mirabelle thought it sounded a warmer destination, but it turned out not to be much better than the garden. Sister Gabriel was old, a wizened little woman with a face like a witch, all crumpled and creased, but when Sister Bernadette handed Mirabelle over, the old lady's face lit up into a beaming smile and her eyes twinkled and it completely transformed her.

'Oh how lovely, company at last.' She thanked Bernadette, who left immediately. Rubbing her hands together, Mirabelle noticed she had gloves on that had no fingers to them. The old nun explained that planting tiny seeds was difficult with gloved hands, so removing the knitted fingers from them made it easier but the rest of her hands could keep warm. 'Keeps the old rheumatics at bay.' the old nun laughed 'Now, what say we start with a warm cup of tea, then I will show you what to do. Sister Gabriel tottered across to a small table on which sat a small kettle, and spirit burner, and proceeded to make the tea. Sister, chatted to Mirabelle, trying to find out what she knew about gardening or even if she was interested, it appeared not only did she not know anything, but more concerning to the old Nun, was that Mirabelle appeared to have no interest. Sister Gabriel was not daunted, her love of gardening, despite her age and poor health, never deterred her from spending time, if not outside, in her greenhouse.

Mirabelle wrapped her hands round the mug of tea given to her, and watched as the Nun filled each tray with fine soil then carefully picked out these little, tiny seeds and planted them one by one in the soil.

Despite wishing to appear uninterested, Sister Gabriel soon won Mirabelle over when she showed her a tray she'd sown several weeks previously, that now had green shoots and she explained the next stage, which she called, "pricking out".

Over the coming weeks, Mirabelle's behaviour slowly began to change. As to whether this was due to the Nun's teaching, or it was simply that Mirabelle had lost the will to fight, only time would tell.

Once she was used to the routines and disciplines of the Convent, Mother Superior decided it was time for a real baptism of fire. And so it was that on this particular morning of handing out the days chores after breakfast, cold fear struck Mirabelle.

'Fine well, now we come to the street visits. I want Sisters Teresa and Mary-Madeline to do these today. And Sisters, I'd like you to take Mirabelle with you.' The Sisters allotted this duty, glanced at one another, then back to Mother Superior, but neither said anything, a duty was a duty, and none of the Sisters would ever dream of querying it. That rule had Passed Mirabelle by. She looked at Mother Superior, then at the Sisters, and back to Mother.

'What does that mean, Mother Superior?' She asked nervously, her former aggressive demanding speech, a thing of the past.

'That you will accompany the Sisters on their rounds of the streets, looking for anyone, man, woman or child, that may need our help.' Mother hesitated before continuing to explain. 'I will warn you though Mirabelle, there will be sights you come across which will distress you, though I hasten to add, you will in no way be in any danger.'

Mirabelle looked wide eyed at the two nuns she was to accompany. They could see the fear in her eyes and remembered their first experience of the street work, and both immediately tried to reassure her of her safety.

Although it was now May, Sister Teresa advised her to put a shawl on, as the places they would be visiting could still be chilly and damp as the sun rarely reached the dwellings.

They set out on foot, as no cart, let alone carriage would be able to enter the maize of streets for which they were heading.

They walked down the Hackney Road, taking many turnings which lead them into a place known as "Old Nicholl." As they walked deeper into the area, the streets became narrower and darker. Noise from the main road ceased, and the streets grew narrow that they had to walk in single file, turning sideways and walking crab wise. Suddenly, they came out onto a square, which was known as a tenement block. By now

Mirabelle had become quite disorientated after so many left turns. The Nuns stopped, giving Mirabelle time to take in her surroundings. Pressing her hand against her nose and mouth, she looked around. The cobbled square, was a mass of holes, filled with filthy, putrid liquid. Surrounding the square on all sides, rose two and three storey houses. Most had windows, though the panes were either cracked or broken, some covered with rags or paper to keep out the cold. If they were lucky, they had a front door, though none were shut, what was the point when you had nothing to steel. If the door was missing, chances are, it had been used as firewood, what else was there to burn when you were poor and cold.

A carcass of a dead dog lay in one corner, nearby was piled unknown rubbish. Mirabelle lifted her eyes skywards. Thin spirals of grey smoke drifted upwards, as the two nuns made their way towards one house, with the door open, they knocked and went in.

The Sisters were greeted with welcoming smiles, though the occupants, a woman, two ragged children and an incredibly old woman sat making something, though Mirabelle knew not what. The children crawled towards them and Mirabelle to her shame withdraw as she could see, despite the dim light, there was movement about the children's heads, and that could only mean one thing, flees. From the bags the Nuns had been carrying, they drew out bread, a stone bottle of clean water, cheese, some broth, porridge oats and milk. These items were greeted with tearful smiles of appreciation and in return, the woman handed back, three empty stone flagons, which had previously held similar offerings.

As Mirabelle grew used to the dim, smoky atmosphere, she realised the women were making matchboxes, and the children, matches. There were so many boxes waiting to be filled, there was hardly room to move.

Mirabelle was relieved when they left the house, though if she wanted to breath in fresh air, she was sadly disappointed, as the air outside was still as foetid as it had been when they went in.

The next house they went in had two rooms which housed a woman, her husband and six children. The two eldest sons were with their father in the back room making uppers for boots and could not stop as this order had to be completed and delivered by six P.M or they wouldn't be eating the 'morrow. Except that the Sisters had come just in time, and proceeded to take out from another bag, goods as before. This woman got up from the floor where she'd been seated, and kissed the hands of the Nuns, her tears of gratitude running down her face, leaving grimy trails.

As they walked the labyrinth of streets, Mirabelle felt uneasy, as if she was being watched, which she was. The Sisters had long walked these streets and knew about the watchful, suspicious, often hated gazes that followed them. Some were suspicious of the goods they handed out, accusing them of trying to poison them.

Back out onto the main street, costermongers lined the thoroughfare with their barrows selling vegetables, some fruit, eels, cockles and mussels, oysters, rabbits, hare and some meat. Rags, cooking pots, and other paraphernalia, some of which had been stolen.

Some women were selling bunches of flowers, heather, matches and kindling for the fire, others were just begging. Many children had broken limbs, black eyes or bruised faces. Mirabelle was shocked at all she had witnessed, it left her speechless, frightened and heartbroken. On the way home, Sister Teresa gave her some of the background.

Ada, a widow who looked after her aged mother and two children, would be paid tuppence farthing for every gross of match boxes, and she would have to make eight gross a day, around one shilling and sixpence a day. Her rent would be about two shilling and threepence a week. She would have to collect wood, labels and sandpaper from the Bryant & May depot to make the boxes and matches and the glue, for which she would have to pay. Death was a blessing in such places.

Mirabelle listened to this in silence, a feeling of such sorrow and desolation coming over her, all she wanted to do on her return, was to retire to bed and sob.

When Sister Mary-Madeline reported back to Mother Superior, they both felt harsh though it may have been for Mirabelle, the girl had taken it all in with remarkable stoicism.

The next stepmother Superior said, would be a visit to the workhouse, and to the hospital. But in view of the experiences of this day, they would wait awhile.

At breakfast the next day, Mirabelle was relieved to find she'd been put back on duty in the kitchen, on bread making.

It was a week before Mirabelle had her next experience of the East End of London life, and that was on the following Sunday, when she was told she would be going with six other of the nuns, to conduct services to those in the workhouse which included a Sunday school for the children. She was sure that nothing could be worse than the street visits, for which she still had nightmares.

She had heard about the workhouses and wondered if the one they were approaching would be as bad as the poverty she'd seen in Old Nicholl. They had walked about a mile, when an enormous three storey, red brick building came into view. Despite it being a sunny day, the huge building gave off an austere atmosphere as they approached. It was surrounded by an eight-foot-high brick wall and through the bars of its iron double gates, the top floor windows had bars in front of them.
As the Nuns approached, a man suddenly appeared and began to unlock the iron chain that held fast the gates. As he opened them, he did not look them in the eye, but instead grunted in response to the nuns cheerful greeting of 'Good Morning'
Mirabelle cast a glance around the grounds which were extensive. Everywhere seemed to support vegetables or what she now knew to be compost heaps, which in the height of summer would give off pungent smells of rotting vegetation, straw and some animal excrement, especially if the kept, pigs, chickens or cows.
The heavy studded oak doors were opened before they reached the bottom step, and a rather austere woman stood ramrod straight, her arms folded across her chest. She wore a grey, no-nonsense dress which was covered by a spotless white full-length apron and on her head, a frilly white cap. She inclined her head in greeting, saying Good Morning, and stepping aside to let them in. They were shown to a room.
'Good Morning Matron, and how are you today?' Sister Mary-Madeline greeted her.
'Good Morning Sisters, I'm very well thank you, all the better for seeing the sunshine. And who is this you have with you?'
'Matron, may I introduce Miss Mirabelle Fanshaw, Miss Fanshaw is joining us at the Sisters of Mercy to learn of the work we do.' Sister Mary-Madeline explained tactfully.

Despite her appearance, Matron's tone was quite congenial and she smiled at Mirabelle, who returned her acknowledgement politely.

'And what have you learned during your stay Miss Fanshaw?' she asked Mirabelle who had not expected to be spoken too, for a moment she was tongue-tied.

'Em....em, well, I have learnt to make bread, gardening and visited the poor in Old Nicholl.' she stammered.

'Old Nicholl! My, my.' Matron said in some surprise. 'And what did you find in Old Nicholl? Were you not frightened?'

A slight shudder passed over her as she remembered what she'd seen. 'Yes Matron, I was. Very frightened.' And as an afterthought she added. 'And very sad, that some people, despite the willingness to work, are unable too, except work that pays them so little, they still have hardly enough to eat, keep warm or even have a decent room to live in.' Mirabelle was warming to her subject and the Nuns cast glances at each other, my goodness, she had taken in all they'd taught her.

'So you realise that not all of those who end up in the workhouse, are miscreants?' Matron said

Mirabelle wasn't sure she knew what the word "Miscreants" meant, but she had an idea, so agreed with Matron.

'And this is your first visit to a workhouse Miss Fanshaw?'

'Yes Matron.'

'And do you know anything about them?'

'Not really Matron.'

'So you haven't read any of the accounts written by Mr Dickens?'

'Who?'

'Mr Dickens, Mr Charles Dickens.'

Mirabelle shook her head slowly, was Matron testing her in some way. She looked to the Nuns for help.

'I don't think Mirabelle has read any of his work Matron.' Sister Mary-Madeline said quickly coming to her aid.

Matron sniffed. 'Probably just as well as the poor child would have been terrified to step over our threshold.' She said turning and walking out of her office and down the corridor. At the end, she turned to speak to the Sisters. 'I will leave you here Sisters, you know where you want to go. But perhaps as Miss Fanshaw has never been to a workhouse before, perhaps I may be permitted to show her round and explain how this workhouse works before Mr Dickens gets chance to disillusion her completely.' She muttered the last under her breath.

'I think that an excellent idea Matron.' Mary-Madeline agreed

Initially, Mirabelle was unsure about this sudden arrangement but relaxed after Matron turned and said. 'I will show you around, tell you how we help people, and then later, we can meet up with the children and workers in the dining hall where on Sunday we have a special treat of hot chocolate.' Matron's face softened at this last, which put Mirabelle at her ease.

Mirabelle followed Matron down yet another corridor after leaving the Nuns. All was silent, except for the occasional muted voice. Abruptly coming to a standstill, Matron pulled at the long silver chain hanging from her waist which had an odd assortment of keys and other paraphernalia hanging from it. Mirabelle recognised this as something similar Mrs Green had worn about her waist, but with far less items.

After spending some time following Matron as she explained to Mirabelle how the unfortunate soles housed within came to be here, they started their tour.

Matron told her that not all workhouses were as well run as hers. It was all down to the governing body, a group of mostly men, who met once a month to talk about the running of such an institution.

Mirabelle heard how there was a Labour Master and a Labour Mistress, who organised the work. There was a laundry, where women would learn to wash and iron their clothes and bedding, a sewing room where they would learn to sew and mend and generally take care of their clothes and bed linen. A kitchen where they would learn to bake bread, and cook good broths and stews, meat was limited, but good, wholesome food could be made using only vegetables, and grains if a few herbs were added. Of course this was women's work.

For the men, the Labour Master would set them on to the garden, where they would learn to till the soil, and grow food for their families, God willing if they should be lucky enough to have a patch of land.

They would learn how to care for chicken, pigs, cows, and the women would be taught to milk a cow, make butter and cheese. Pluck and gut, chickens, skin and gut hares and rabbits, though they were not encouraged to poach, not that there was much chance of that in London.

All children were taught the three R's reading, writing and arithmetic. In the hope that in time, there would be a possibility work could be found for them when they were old enough. These children could be found work in good houses as servants because of their education and learnt skills. At thirteen, the boys could be apprenticed, or sent for training in the Royal Navy, always with the watchful eye of the guardians to ensure no mistreatment occurred. Not all workhouses were as generous as this. Matron told her.

In this workhouse, Matron said, sick, elderly and women with child, many young ones, unmarried and thrown out of their homes, would be looked after and not abused as in many workhouses.

Mirabelle listened to all this thinking how lucky they could be in comparison to those living in Old Nicholl.

'What did you mean about that man, that Mr Dickens?' Mirabelle asked curious as she had never heard of him.

'Charles Dickens writes stories about workhouses, one such is called 'Oliver Twist', it is a very gruesome work, about an orphan boy born and brought up in a workhouse.' Matron sighed heavily.

'He describes the very worst of such places, with cruel Masters and even crueller Governors. Sadly, such places do exist.

'What happens in those other places?'

'Beatings, tasteless, poor-quality food, dirty surroundings and children, often sold or hired out to be sent down mines or to work in factories.' Matron held off adding, sexual abuse, fearing a young lady of Mirabelle's delicate ears would be too shocked.

Having been shown around where all the activities took place, the dormitories where they slept, they made their way to the dining hall where the Nuns, having finished their services and Sunday School teachings, awaited their arrival to enjoy the hot chocolate, promised by Matron.

Mirabelle was impressed as they entered, the children and adults stood, then sat down when matron and the nuns did.

On the way back to the Convent, Mirabelle was full of what she'd learnt and asked the question, why are not all workhouses run like the one they'd visited, back came the answer given earlier by Matron, the Governors.

'But they should be sacked!' Cried Mirabelle indignantly.

The Nuns smiled, if only it was as easy as that. Trouble was it had a lot to do with money, money and greed.

CHAPTER 11

Mirabelle's visit to the workhouse played heavily on her mind. She was beginning to think about her own life and questioned why she'd been so horrible. She wanted to talk to her Papa, to say how sorry she was and hope that he would still love her. More than anything now she wanted to be loved, and that wasn't far off, though not in the way she would have expected.

She resolved to write to Papa and beg his forgiveness, tell him all that she'd seen and to that end, she asked Mother Superior at breakfast that morning, if she could have pen and paper so she may write to her Papa. Mother said she could have it that evening after supper when they returned from St Thomas' hospital.

This was to be another knew experience, and she had heard of Miss Florence Nightingale.

'Is this the hospital that Miss Nightingale works at?' She asked when Mother Superior said she was to go with Sisters Bernadette and Gabriel to St Thomas.'

'Ah, I see you have heard of Miss Nightingale, and what do you know of her work?'

'Not a lot actually. The only reason I've heard of her, was when I was "Coming Out", many of Mama's friends were scandalised, and we debutantes' were not supposed to hear about her "goings on," as they put it.'

'And now? What are your thoughts?' Mother asked. Mirabelle shrugged. 'Well, I very much doubt you will have the honour of meeting the lady herself, as recently she accepted the position of Superintendent in Upper Harley Street, for the care of sick Gentlewomen.'

'But what about the poor and the sick of London, does she not care? That is not what I understood.'

Mother shook her head. 'Oh she cares well enough. She campaigns for better sanitation, better nutrition, and tries desperately to instil cleanliness in hospitals by way of teaching those who nurse, to scrub their hands, wash thoroughly and boil instruments when dealing with patients. But she needs better educated women to work alongside her, and as you have just said, ladies such as she are not encouraged to work alongside her. Why, even her own parents were scandalised when she took up the mantle.' Mother breathed a heavy sigh, 'No my dear, it will be some time before we have more ladies like Miss Nightingale. I do think though, that by taking on the position of Superintendent, that she is hoping to show to those who oppose her, that her work is worthwhile and as she heals these Gentlewomen, they will be so grateful to her, that they will join her or encourage others too.'

'Well, I would like to meet her.' Mirabelle said

'And I hope one day you will, but in the meantime, you could do a lot of good on her behalf. If you spread the word, and be seen to practice her teachings, think what that would do for her cause.'

With this in mind, Mirabelle set off with the two Sisters for St Thomas' the following day. Because of the distance, they were obliged to take the horse and cart, but Mirabelle was now used to Tom's cheeky, chirpy chatter, as since that first time when he'd collected them from the railway station on her arrival, she'd seen him often, and now automatically gave him a cheerful wave.

As they made their way to their destination, the two Sisters, conversed freely with young Tom. Mirabelle was deep in thought. She was restless, there was a new urgency about her, but she didn't know what it was. Arriving at the Hospital, they left Tom, who promised to be back at four P.M. to take them back.Climbing the stairs and going through the double doors, Mirabelle was assailed with a musty smell. 'I thought Miss Nightingale had already started on the importance of cleanliness.' She said. Sister Bernadette smiled.

'You will find that saying it and getting people to carry out your instructions when you are out of sight, are two different things. It will take time, especially with some of the so called "nurses" we have working here, which is why, I have heard Miss Nightingale is keen to set up a nursing school.'

Mirabelle's eyes lit up. 'Really? Oh how wonderful. When will it start?'

'Oh not for some time yet, it's still in the early stages of thought and planning.'

As they made their way through the corridors, Mirabelle was able to peep into the wards where she saw beds that held patients, some engaged in conversation with men in suits, who she thought must be doctors. The women whom she guessed were nurses, were a great disappointment. They didn't look particularly clean, but her thoughts were interrupted when they arrived at Matron's door.

Sister Bernadette introduced Mirabelle, and Matron who smiled a welcome. 'Is there anywhere in particular you would like us to work Matron?' Sister Bernadette asked.

Matron hesitated, looking at Mirabelle, she wasn't sure just how this young woman would stand up to the reality of childbirth. 'Well....., I was going to suggest help on the labour ward, but....'

'No problem at all.' Sister Bernadette answered her briskly. 'Come along Sister Gabriel, Mirabelle, follow me, I know the way.'

To Mirabelle, the word "Labour" meant only one thing, work, so she was surprised when she walked into a ward to find a young woman writhing in pain. Taking some gowns off the hooks, Sister Bernadette threw them down angrily. 'These are of no use whatsoever, they're filthy!' Looking around, she saw a woman skulking in a cupboard. 'You there,' She advanced on the woman who retreated further into the cupboard. 'Are there no clean gowns to be had?' The woman turned and pointed to shelves, whereupon lay a pile of clean linen, including gowns. Bernadette reached for three handing one to Mirabelle and one to Gabriel. Going towards the patient, Bernadette called for the woman to bring her clean sheets and a gown for the young woman. ' Now, Mirabelle, help me strip this bed and this young woman of her soiled clothes, Sister Gabriel, fetch a bowl of warm water, soap and towels. And you,' She pointed to the woman who seemed frozen on the spot, staring wildly at the Nun as if she'd never seen one before. 'What is your name?'

'Phoebe, Madam, Miss, your worship,......' She whispered

'Sister, will do Phoebe. Now, when we have removed this bedding, I want you to take it all down to the wash house, including those gowns I've just removed, and have it laundered immediately, do you understand?'

'Yes Mi...Sister.'

'How long have you worked here Phoebe?'

'Just today Mi, Sister, I just come see, and Matron told me, stay here and someone will come and tell you what to do, but no-one come see.'

'I see. Well that was unfortunate. Do you know where the wash house is?' Sister Bernadette tried to sound less sharp.

'No Mi.... Sister.'

Just then someone else walked passed the ward, Sister Bernadette called out, 'You there, come here.' Another woman appeared at the door looking annoyed at being commanded, but when she recognised the Nun's uniform, inclined her head saying. 'Yes Sister?'

'Do you know where the wash house is?'

'Should do, I just come from there.'

'Good, please take Phoebe here and show her, then instruct her on how to wash this soiled linen. Then I would be grateful if you can find us fresh linen to restock the cupboard.'

'Hey, just a minute, you can't come in 'ere shoutin' the odds and tellin' us what to do, that's Matron's job!'

Suddenly from the bed came a cry for help. 'Will you lot stop bleedin arguing, I'm layin' 'ere bleedin freezing!'

Bernadette turned back to her patient and continued gently to bathe her but not before turning her gaze on the woman standing beside her and shouted. 'Just do it!' she was about to argue when in walked a man, who backed Sister Bernadette's instructions.

'Please do as the Sister asks you, she and her Sisters are here to help and their time is given voluntarily, I therefore expect you and everyone else working here, to respect them.'

'Yes Doctor.' The woman almost gave a little bow, then turning to Phoebe said. 'Come on then, pick that lot up, I aint got all day.'

The doctor approached them and his patient. 'Good Morning Sisters, Miss,' He addressed Mirabelle, then back to his patient. 'Ah, I see you are bathing Mrs Caplin, good, and you will soon have a nice clean bed to lie on. You will feel much better, more comfortable.'

'I'll feel' a lot more comfortable when this little bleeder is born...ooowww.'

'Well I will examine you in a moment. I'm sorry I haven't introduced myself Sisters, I am Doctor Raj Patel, and from what I am observing, you are acquainted with the teachings of Miss Nightingale'

'We are indeed Doctor, though cleanliness is something we have always adhered to.'

'I am sure it is Sister but thank you for helping Mrs Caplin. Now, let's see how we are doing.'

'If you do not need us Doctor, we will carry on in the other ward.'

'Yes that's fine, though I would be grateful if one of you could stay, I'm sure Mrs Caplin would appreciate the company.'

Sister Bernadette looked from one to the other, Mirabelle spoke. 'I'll stay Sister.'

Surprised, Bernadette said, 'Come along then Sister Gabriel, we will be back later for you Mirabelle.'

As soon as they'd left, Mrs Caplin started to writhe about once again. Mirabelle immediately took hold of her hand, stroking it gently, making soft, cooing noises, to calm her. Doctor Patel looked up, impressed. 'I see you have done this before?' He suggested quietly. Mirabelle shook her head slowly in denial, turning to speak to him she was struck dumb. She was gripped as their eyes met. He had the most beautiful dark brown eyes she had ever seen. They were soft and as she gazed at him they reminded her of warm, dark chocolate. For the first time she noticed his skin, it was the colour of milky coffee, and black curls fell on to his forehead. But she wasn't the only one to be stunned. Raj's heart skipped a beat as he looked into the sweetest face he'd ever seen. Her clear blue eyes were so full of compassion, and her skin alabaster pale which contrasted with her red gold curls, that had escaped from the small white cap she wore upon her head.

'When you two luv birds 'ave stooped gazing at each uver like a couple of sick parrots, I'm abart to give birf!   ggrrrrrrrrr' and within minutes, the baby was born.

As doctor Patel dealt with mother and child, Mirabelle felt she needed to get away as quickly as possible, what had happened to them just now, for she felt it wasn't just she who had been affected. Doctor Patel had felt the same, she was sure he had. Mirabelle was to say his name over and over again, Doctor Raj Patel, Doctor Raj Patel, she was captivated and if only she knew it, so was he.

That evening, after supper and evensong, Mirabelle sat down to write the long overdue letter to her Papa. As she wrote, Mother Superior was also busy writing a letter to Lord Fanshaw.

Sisters of Mercy Convent
Elman Street
Hackney
London
September 9th, 1856

Dearest Papa

First, I must apologise for my delay in writing, so much has happened since arriving here. I will try to tell you of all I have seen and done but there is so much, and I may find it hard to describe. I would love to tell you so I am hoping you may consider a visit to London. I have learnt so many things, I can now make bread, and make a bed, so tell Poppy she will have little to do when I return home. Papa, I have seen such scenes, that should I describe them you would think I had taken them from reading one of the stories of Mr Charles Dickens, who is well known in these parts.

Please give my love to Teddy, how is he?

Your loving daughter,

Mirabelle

Sisters of Mercy Convent
Elman Street
Hackney
London
9ᵗʰ September 1856

Dear Lord Fanshaw
I understand that Mirabelle is writing to you this very evening, so I thought it was time to put in another report. I am incredibly happy to say that since my previous missive, Mirabelle is quite the changed young Lady. I think you will be enormously proud of her; we certainly are.
Mirabelle has tackled all kinds of work, some very unpleasant and met some difficult situations and although she has struggled, she has not shied away. I know she would love to see you so if you would care to make a visit, you would be most welcome.

Yours truly,

Mother Superior

The following morning, Mother handed both letters to Tom requesting he take them to the post office.

The letters arrived together a few days later and Henry-Carmichael was delighted when he read them. Had it not been for Mother Superior's report, he might have been reluctant to believe all he read of Mirabelle's letter. Could it really be true, that his troublesome daughter had really changed. He would have to go to London and the sooner the better. He went out to find McGregor, to tell him he would be away for a few days from Monday, but before then, he would visit Shelagh, and show her the letters, see what she thought, though he couldn't help feeling excited. A smile played on his lips, and he prayed he'd really got his daughter back, like the little girl she had once been.

When Shelagh heard a horse clip clopping down the lane, she was pleased when looking out of her window she saw Henry approaching.

'You look very pleased with yourself, have you had some good news?'

'Yes, a letter, well two in fact, one from Mother Superior, and the other from Mirabelle.'

'Oh? I thought you were going to say it was from Teddy. Is Mirabelle asking to come home?'

'No, it appears not. On the contrary, she seems to be thriving on her good works.'

'Good works! Mirabelle?' Shelagh asked, shocked.'

Henry was beaming with pride. 'Here, read for yourself.' He said handing over the two letters.

Shelagh glanced and said 'Right, you sit down, I'll make the tea and then I can read them.'

When they were both comfortable and Henry was drinking his tea and eating a slice of seed cake, Shelagh settled down to read the letters. Having read the first, she sat back in surprise, looking at Henry who just smiled and raised an eyebrow. Shelagh turned her attention to the other, and read

'I don't know what to say. But I agree, if it wasn't for Mother Superior's letter, I too would have had my doubts, but.......well, let's hope this enthusiasm continues. So, what are you going to do now? She makes no mention of returning.'

I'm going to London, Monday. I have spoken to McGregor, and he will hold the fort for me, I have also written to Mother Superior, telling her of my impending visit, and asking her not to inform Mirabelle. I want it to be a surprise.'

Shelagh smiled, nodding in agreement. She hoped that Henry would not be disappointed, two of his children had given him enough grief, she just hoped and prayed this was not some kind of ruse of Mirabelle's to fool her father.

They spent a pleasant afternoon discussing news of Teddy's ongoing achievements at University, Eilish's growing accomplishments at the Emporium of Mrs Wright, and Eamon's ongoing training with Joe Blackstone.

Henry told her he'd seen Eamonn recently, when Joe had brought him to The Hall to shoe one of his horses, and Joe had been full of enthusiasm for the young boy.

'Yes, so much so, that he is now giving Eamonn a small wage, even though his apprenticeship is not complete.' Shelagh told him.

They were so busy talking, they lost track of time, and as the sun started to go down, Eamonn arrived home from work.

'Good heavens, is that the time?' Shelagh started.

Henry jumped up. 'I'm so sorry, I fear I have held you up.'

'No, no, please, I have enjoyed our crack.' Shelagh said using the Irish for talk. Turning to Eamonn Henry said.

'If your supper is delayed, I am afraid it is all my fault.'

Eamonn smiled, he liked Lord Fanshaw. 'No problem Sir, It's nice for the Mammy to have some company, it must be awful lonely for her with me out all day and Eilish only at home on a Sunday.'

'Oh get away with you. ' Shelagh said playfully. 'I've always got plenty to do, which reminds me, I've a pot of home-made apricot jam for you to take back to The Hall, I hope Cook won't be offended.' She said going to the cupboard and taking out a jar. 'We've had so many apricots this year it's been a bumper year. The tree loves it up against that wall, your gardener gave me that tip, "Train it along that wall Misses." he told me, "The warmth of the sun on that there bricks will warm them and encourage 'em to grow", and do you know what? He was right.' Shelagh laughed.

'Yes, we have stewed apricots with our porridge, fresh apricots in my lunch box and apricot tart for supper!' Eamonn teased his mother.

'Yes, well I will look forward to having this on my toast in the morning, so thank you, and don't worry about cook, she'll probably bless you.' Henry said waving the jar aloft.

'Good luck on Monday.' Shelagh called out after him as he made his way back down the front path.

'I will let you know how I get on.'

'You do that.'

'What was that all about?' Eamonn asked, and Shelagh told him about the letters and his Lordships pending trip to London, as she prepared supper.

CHAPTER 12

Henry-Carmichael's journey to London had been unremarkable. He'd been there several times, and on these new-fangled trains which he could see would revolutionise travel. Though thinking of his daughter's first experience back in March, it must have been one of fear, but with the two Nuns by her side, he hoped she had not been too frightened.

On his arrival in London, he hired a carriage to take him first to his hotel, and after registering, on to the Sisters of Mercy Convent.

It was late when he eventually arrived, pulling on the bell-rope. Evensong was over and supper finished, but Mother Superior was not concerned, having him brought straight to her office and sending a nun to ask cook to arrange a tray of supper for him.

They talked for a little while, she asking about his journey, and he saying how delighted he was to receive her letter and the one from Mirabelle. He wondered why she looked uncomfortable when he mentioned his daughters name and wondered why Mother had not sent for her. 'Is everything alright? He enquired.

'Oh dear, Lord Fanshaw. I do apologise, but Mirabelle is not here at present.'

'Not here? What do you mean?' At first he feared something dreadful had happened, but Mother Superior was quick to reassure him.

'Oh, it's nothing for you to worry about, I just hope I haven't done the wrong thing. You see, Mirabelle has taken to working at St Thomas' hospital. She first went there as part of our varied duties within the East End, but it seems she has found.........well, I'm not sure what to call it.

Vocation at this stage might seem a little too strong a word, but she certainly has shown an affinity with the work within the hospital.' She was about to add a bit more but thought better of it, it may be her imagination, but if she were asked she might have said, maybe there was an added attraction of a certain Doctor.

'I see.' Lord Fanshaw said, and Mother was pleased to see he was smiling. Would he be smiling when she told him the rest. 'But surely it's late to be working isn't it?'

'Oh no, she is not working tonight, you see Charles Dickens the writer, is giving a reading tonight at the hospital. It is to entertain the patients and raise funds for the hospital. One of the Doctors, a Doctor Raj Patel, asked if Mirabelle would like to hear him, she said yes, although not before asking my permission, and Sister Abigail is also staying. Doctor Patel promised to bring them home by carriage at the end of the evening. I do hope my action holds with your approval?' She finished hesitantly.

'I think I'm rather delighted, Mother Superior. I think it an excellent idea. It's good to see my daughter taking such an interest, I wouldn't mind hearing the gentleman myself. My son Teddy is a great fan of Mr Dickens.'

Mother Superior relaxed. Just then the doorbell rang. 'Ah, I think that maybe them now.'

There was a flurry of excited voices and footsteps hurrying to Mother Superiors office. A quick knock, and the door flew open, and an excited Mirabelle entered the room followed by a Nun and a dark-skinned gentleman, no one noticed Lord Fanshaw sitting there in the corner, as he finished his supper.

'Oh Mother Superior, it was wonderful! He read passages from Oliver Twist and Domby and Son, and his latest story, Bleak House, which has been serialised, and is to be published as a book. I think I am going to buy it for my brother Teddy, he loves Mr Dickens..........'She stopped as she could see Mother Superior trying not laugh, then followed her gaze as she looked across the room where a gentleman was sitting, obviously having just finished a meal. For a moment she started, not recognising him in the gloom of Mother's office. Then recognition fell upon her.

'Papa! She cried in delight and rushed towards him. 'What brings you here?'

Laughing. Henry-Carmichael stood and gathered his daughter to him as she ran too him. 'To see you my dear, to see you.'

'Oh Papa, if I had known you were coming I would have been here to greet you.'

'Well then I am glad you didn't. I would not have wanted to spoil your evening, which you have undoubtedly enjoyed.'

Suddenly, Mirabelle remembered her manners. 'Oh Papa, Raj, I'm so sorry. Papa, may I introduce Doctor Raj Patel, Doctor Patel, my Papa, Lord Fanshaw.' Henry-Carmichael stood up and greeted the young doctor, who he took an instant liking too, recognising he wasn't the only one. Well, if this young man had anything to do with this new daughter that stood before him, then who was he to complain, of course, society would not agree.

'I am honoured to meet you Sir.' Raj said

'And I you, Doctor Patel.'

'And Papa, this is Sister Abigail, who kindly attended with me for the evening, and Ra...Doctor Patel, you know Mother Superior.'

'I do indeed and thank you Mother Superior for allowing the ladies to attend the reading, I think we all enjoyed it immensely. Now I must bid you all a good evening.'

Sister Abigail said goodnight and showed Raj out. Mother asked if his Lordship would like to go to the lounge to talk with his daughter and he said he would, but not keep her too long as they all needed to get to bed, and he to his hotel.

Father and daughter chatted, and he was overcome with joy at the change in his daughter. 'Mother Superior tells me you are a keen attendee at St Thomas?'

'Yes Papa, Oh the things I've seen Papa, it has been heart-breaking.'

'Well, you can tell me all about it tomorrow.'

'How long are you staying Papa?' Mirabelle asked eagerly.

'Just for a few days, I just wanted to see you and know that you are well.'

'Oh I am Papa, I am.'

'Good, and I can see that and I'm so very happy for you my dear.' Leaning to kiss his daughter goodbye, he said. 'Until tomorrow, perhaps we can go somewhere for lunch and you can tell me all your news.'

'Oh yes Papa, I will look forward to that.' Mirabelle showed him out then went to bed, a happy young woman, happier than ever that her Papa had seemed pleased to meet her beloved Raj and appeared not to blink an eyelid!

At ten O'clock the following morning, Lord Fanshaw was at the door of the convent with a carriage. They headed for the West End, as he thought a little shopping trip to Harrods and Fortnum and Masons before lunch at Browns Hotel, would be a treat for Mirabelle.

He was surprised at Mirabelle, who though enthusiastic in the items she saw in the stores, seemed little interested in buying anything. When asked about this, she replied. 'Papa, I have so many outfits and accessories, there is nothing I require. But thank you anyway.'

She went on to tell him about her first visit to Old Nicholl, and he was horrified and fascinated at the same time of her description, and her compassion for the people she'd met.

'And I understand you have been helping at St Thomas'?'

'Yes Papa, have you heard of Miss Nightingale, Florence Nightingale?'

'I think everyone has heard of Miss Nightingale, much to the distress of her family.'

'Well they shouldn't feel distress, they should be proud of what she is achieving. Do you know Papa, she is already proving her advice about hygiene is correct, and the Nuns follow her teachings. The first time I went to the hospital Sister Bernadette was furious when we went to the labour ward, there was only one young woman in labour, so they had no excuse they were too busy, yet the poor thing was laying in dirty, soiled bedding. Sister immediately instructed a woman standing around, to bring clean sheets and a gown, and to take the dirty laundry and get them into the wash tubs. Then Doctor Patel arrived, and I could tell he was impressed with Sister's instructions.'

'And this would be the Doctor Patel that took you and Sister Abigail to hear Mr Dickens read.'

'Yes Papa, we got to talking about the workhouses, and I told him how I had been to one and had been pleasantly surprised, he said, "You obviously haven't read any of Mr Dickens works" I had to confess I had not but told him my brother Teddy was a great fan.' She bubbled on much to the amusement of her father.

'And Doctor Patel? What can you tell me about him? You seen to be rather friendly towards the gentleman?'

'Oh Papa,' Mirabelle tried to hide her blushes. 'I can assure you, there is nothing untoward, he has always behaved impeccably, but he is such an interesting man, and I am ashamed to say, he knows more about English history than I!'

'Does he indeed.' Her Papa replied doing his best to hide a little smile, though at the same time wondering if apart from amusement, should he not be a little concerned, after all, his daughter was an impressionable girl, young and inexperienced in matters of the heart, if this friendship was veering in that direction.........?

'His parents sent him to England when he was a small boy, knowing he would get a better education and a chance, when he was older to study and become a Doctor.'

'He must have been very young.'

'He was, the youngest in a family of seven, all six before him, girls!' She giggled

'Oh dear, expensive for his Papa.' He said

Mirabelle shook her head. 'Not really. His father is a Maharajah and very wealthy, but his deepest wish was that Rajiv became a Doctor. Do you know there are thirty-three main Gods and Goddesses in the Hindu religion, the three main ones being, Brahma, Vishnu and Shiva, and many Hindu's do not eat meat.'

The more Mirabelle talked about Raj Patel, the more she warmed to her subject and Henry-Carmichael started to grow a little alarmed.

What if the doctor was expected to return to India in time, his daughter could not possibly go with him, she would never be accepted. He told himself, this was just a girlish fascination for someone of a different culture, whom she admired and respected, nothing more.

The three days Lord Fanshaw spent in London, were soon over. He'd spent each day with Mirabelle and in the evening they had gone once to the theatre, and on another, had dined with friends at their home in Mayfair. These friends had not seen Mirabelle since her disastrous "Coming out" and couldn't believe the change in little over a year.
Gone was the fat, frumpy, sulky, young woman and in her place was a slim, pretty, articulate and interesting young woman you could converse intelligently. Though she did rather shock when talking about the state of the living standards in the East End, workhouses, and an Indian Doctor by the name of Raj Patel. However, they did warm to her when she mentioned the teachings of the Nuns, Miss Nightingale, and when she told them of her visit to hear Mr Dickens read, they were greatly impressed.

All too soon it was time for Henry-Carmichael to say goodbye to his daughter, confirming that she would return to Wynchampton in time for Christmas. He would send Poppy to London to escort her home but did not add that he hoped she would stay, though it did cross his mind she might find Wynchampton rather boring.

When Lord Fanshaw arrived home, he was greeted with enthusiasm by all his servants. He was a much like and respected employer. A letter awaited him from Teddy, announcing he would be home from university for the half term in October.
He replied immediately telling his son how much he was looking forward to seeing him and telling him the wonderful news of the changes to come over Mirabelle, who now he considered utterly charming. Although he mentioned some of her experiences, he left out the details of Doctor Patel. He did not dislike the young Doctor, on the

contrary, he liked and admired the young man immensely. He resolved to pay Shelagh a visit and ask her advice.

The following morning he rode into Oxford, and having posted his letter, called at Mrs Wrights' emporium. Mrs Wright greeted him warmly and having shown him around the new extension, invited him to take lunch with her.
She told him all about purchasing the shop next door, which was now a milliners, on the ground floor and on the one above was now a workshop where she employed milliners to create hats exclusive to Wrights' Emporium.
Eilish, Mrs Wright informed him, was her right-hand assistant, now responsible for buying a great deal of the stock. Mrs Wright now owned three large shops which had all been knocked into one, making one large department store, but she was not finished yet. The first and original was still a haberdashery, but also sported a dressmaking service, to the right of this, they now sold beautiful, hand-made rugs and carpets, many imported from India and China, and to the left was the milliners. Mrs Wright had her sights on the rather large corner shop next door, presently an Ironmongers. The old gent who owned it had promised her and Mr Wright, first refusal when he retired. She intended to renovate and have high class furniture for every room in a home, her husband would run this department and would cease travelling quite so much. And Eilish, she confided in him, would have a big part to play in her plans. He was pleased that Eilish had established herself with Mrs Wright, who clearly had taken to the young girl.
'Come, Lord Fanshaw,' she said when they had finished lunch. 'We will go and find Eilish, and you will see for yourself how well she is doing.'
'They waited in the background as Eilish helped one of the servants with a lady who was enquiring about an outfit and a hat to be made for a grand affair she would be attending.
As Lord Fanshaw watched and listened, he couldn't have been more proud of Eilish if she had been his own daughter. He couldn't wait to see her mother.

It was rather late by the time Lord Fanshaw arrived back in Wynchampton, so he decided to delay his call on Shelagh until the following day.

He was feeling in buoyant mood, after his successful visit to London, and with the recent letter from Teddy, family life seemed to be settling down to a more peaceful period.

Then he was brought back to earth with a thud. As he settled in his study to enjoy a pre-dinner drink and read the days post, he saw an official looking letter with Army logo on the envelope. Slitting open the envelope, he was devastated to read an appalling report on Josephs' behaviour. The only saving grace was, that unlike previous schools and university, the Army refused to give up and made it clear that despite everything, they would make an honourable gentleman of him yet, 'Or die in the attempt.' He muttered to himself. It was a bitter blow, what had he done that his eldest son should behave continually in a way that was so socially unacceptable?

As he rode out the following morning, he felt the first nip in the air, the promise of Autumn.

Smoke spiralled out of Shelagh's chimney, and he was looking forward to a hot chocolate and something nice to eat, as Shelagh either had scones, or griddled cakes on offer. He wasn't disappointed. Knocking on the door, it was swiftly opened. 'Good Morning Henry, come on in out of the cold. October is no sooner upon us than the cold winds remind us that Summer is behind us.'

'It does indeed.' He said rubbing his hands and making his way towards the log fire.

'How have you been, and how was your trip to London?' Shelagh asked.

Henry seated himself, smiling as he recalled Shelagh's greeting, she easily called him Henry these days. He shook his head, still beaming. 'I cannot tell you Shelagh how Mirabelle has changed. If I didn't know better, I would have said someone had snatched my daughter and replaced her with an angel. Not only has she changed in her behaviour and attitude, she has slimmed down and looks utterly beautiful. I have only one concern and that is, she has taken to life in London with such enthusiasm, I am concerned she may find life back at The Hall, boring.'

'You mean she is socialising?' Shelagh asked

'No, no nothing like that. On the contrary, she has been helping the Nuns with their work.' Shelagh frowned, this didn't sound like the girl she knew. 'She has been visiting workhouses, the slums of the East End, delivering food and clothes. She even visits St. Thomas', the hospital, where she regularly helps, and is a great fan of Miss Nightingale......' he hesitated, and Shelagh sensed a 'but'. Putting her head on one side, she raised a questioning eyebrow. 'There is one thing that concerns me.....'

'Oh?'

Mirabelle seems to be.......well, I don't know how to put it, she seems to be enamoured with a certain gentleman.'

'Oh?' Shelagh repeated 'And that is not good news? Is he unsuitable?'

'He's a Doctor and an extremely eligible young man, I liked him very much.'

'So what is the objection?' Shelagh asked mystified.

'He's an Indian Doctor.....' Shelagh gasped, not because she had dislikes for the Doctors of another colour or culture but because she and her family had suffered discrimination and she was surprised that Henry too felt this way. She also worried that she too had news he might not like. But he was quick to reassure her, she had misunderstood him.

'No, nothing like that. I am just concerned he may want to return to his own country and practice there. I dread to think that Mirabelle may want to follow him, and I doubt she could possibly be accepted.' He explained, concerned.

Shelagh offered him a griddled cake as he drank the hot chocolate. She sighed heavily trying to find the words to comfort him. 'As long as it is not a class clash on your mind, after all, I'm sure our friendship, is often talked about and disagreed with.'

Henry sat up straight. 'No my dear, absolutely not. My only concern is Mirabelle's happiness. And as for us....'

'Yes, there is us. And I think before we go any further, I should tell you something.' Shelagh looked uncomfortable and licking her lips, decided to come out with it. There would be no point in going round in circles. 'It's about Eilish....' But before she could continue, Henry interrupted her.

'Oh yes, and talking of Eilish, I called at Mrs Wright's Emporium yesterday, and she was showing me around and telling me of her plans, which I am pleased to say, included Eilish. Mrs Wright is extremely impressed with her work and I managed to have a chat with your daughter, and she seems to be incredibly happy. I thought of how proud you must be of her, I certainly would be if she were mine.' He finished. Shelagh took a deep breath. How would he react when he heard what she was about to say?

'Well, I hope you will still feel the same when I tell you about my visitor.'

'Oh....?'

'Have you heard from Teddy lately?' Shelagh asked

'Yes, as a matter of fact I received a letter from him just before leaving to visit Mirabelle. He seemed to be doing well and said he would be home for half-term and again for Christmas. Why do you ask?'

'I too had a letter from him, asking if he might call, which he did while you were in London. It seems that Teddy and Eilish have been writing to each other since the beginning of the year. Something they agreed to do after we'd spent Christmas day afternoon together.. It appears they have had the occasional meeting in Oxford, which has included an afternoon visit to a tea shop and boating on the river would you believe. He apologised for not gaining my permission beforehand for these outings, but apparently they were of a "sudden impulse", so he tells me. The reason for his visit, was to ask my permission to "walk out" with my daughter, and that his intentions, despite his youth, were as he put it "entirely honourable!"

Henry sat back stunned. Not that Teddy had taken a real liking for Eilish, but that he'd chosen to be so outspoken about it. He didn't know what to say. Was it possible that Teddy had really thought this out?

What of his future as Lord of the Manor? And did Eilish realise how different her life would be.

Shelagh was watching Henry's reaction but unable to gage it, she waited. 'Well?' She asked having waited and not received any comment.

Henry smiled. 'Well, I think if Eilish is brave enough to join our family, Teddy could have no better wife, I take it that is where this is leading?'

Shelagh shrugged, 'They're young yet, it might all fizzle out. Perhaps they have mistaken friendship for something else.'

Henry nodded sagely. 'Perhaps. Though I must say, I can see them together. I think they would make a fine pair. And it would be a great relief for me to know The Hall was in such capable hands. Would you have any objections?' he asked

Shelagh thought about it, knowing they would have Henry's blessing. She smiled. 'What Mother wouldn't welcome a young man like Teddy to take care of her daughter.

PART THREE

And Finally

April 1860

CHAPTER 13

'Phillips is here to see you your Lordship, he says you sent for him Sir.'

'Yes that's right Stanley, show him in.' Harold Stanley stood back opening Lord Fanshaw's study door and ushered in the handyman.

'His Lordship will see you now.' He said

Edgar Phillips entered the room, twisting his cap in hand, wondering why he'd been summoned.   'Morning' yer Lordship, yer wanted ta see me Sir.'

'Ah Phillips, yes come in, sit down.' Henry-Carmichael pointed to one of the leather chairs in his   study. Phillips hesitated knowing his work clothes were none to clean. Henry realised his hesitation. 'Oh don't worry about your trousers Phillips, leather can soon be wiped over, sit down, sit down. Would you like some tea, I need to talk to you, get some advice, ideas, you know.' Henry went to the bell pull and when it was answered, asked the maid to bring them tea and biscuits.

Turning to Phillips he said. 'What is the condition of the Dower House do you know?'

Taken aback, Edgar was startled. 'Don't rightly know Sir. Long time since I bin up there.'

'I should imagine it could do with some repairs if it were to be inhabited again.' Edgar nodded in agreement, then found his voice.

'Need to 'ave a good look at it, but chimney's need sweepin', roof probably wants seein' too and garden certainly needs seein' too. Gardeners only just mow lawns to keep it tidy, as fer the inside....well, long time since a body lived there.' He said scratching his head. 'Her

Ladyship, your Mama, was last person to live there, lovely Lady she was an all, begging yer pardon Sir.'

Henry smiled. His Mother had been a real Lady and had only gone to live in the Dower House after he'd married Lucinda, as she couldn't get on with her daughter-in-law, sadly she'd passed away just after Joseph was born. Henry realised he'd drifted off with his thoughts. 'Sorry, Phillips, miles away. As I was saying, I think we should go and have a look at it, make a few notes, see what needs to be done.'

Henry took a walk down to the Dower House later that afternoon. He had an idea, of course it would only work if certain situations took place, and there would be a lot of planning if what he had in mind was to come to fruition. In the meantime, it would do no harm to spruce the place up a bit, starting with the garden.

Looking out from one of the four bedrooms windows, he looked down onto the neglected garden. The trees, apple, plum and a cherry, all had new green shoots. Surrounding the bottom of them, green stalks and leaves waved gently in the breeze, with the promise of daffodils about to bloom. Primroses and other wildflowers were starting to peek through the grass, spring was certainly on its way.

When Lord Fanshaw was joined by Edgar Phillips, they spent time inspecting the house, making notes of urgent jobs to be done, and trades people to be contacted.

Then, to Edgar Phillips surprise, they made their way to the chapel within the grounds of The Hall. 'We need someone to come and tidy this as well.' Henry commented. All his ancestors had been buried there in the cemetery, including his parents and his late wife Lucinda. He had feeling they would be using the chapel with more regularity than they had done so for some years.

'I'll have a word with the gardeners, get them to come up here, and the Dower House, really make the place look nice.

Back at The Hall, Henry was still thoughtful and planning, though before he could take his plans further, there were a number of factors to be considered.

Teddy had qualified in law and was now employed and recently made a partner with his firm, Salter & Salter, now called Salter, Salter & Fanshaw. He had spoken to his father that weekend in regard to his relationship with Eilish. Over the previous four years, their bond had strengthened, so it was no surprise when he asked his father if he had any objections to his speaking to Shelagh in regard to asking for her daughters hand in marriage. This request came as no surprise to him, nor would it to Shelagh when approached.

Mirabelle was also back in the family fold having returned from London some two years previously, having spent much of that time under the tutorial of Miss Nightingale who had taken the post of Superintendent in a Harley Street Practice. By following the notes Miss Nightingale wrote, which was later to become the teachings for training of nurses, Mirabelle was so well thought of, she had returned to Oxford where Doctor Rajiv Patel, had set up a small private hospital, and now the pair, plus assistants ran a well-known and respected practice.

The original funding for the project had come from an inheritance left for Raj by his grandmother and was kept afloat by his well to do patients. These funds enabled the pair to treat many poor and impoverished people in Oxford, to good clean treatments and medicines, free of charge, something that was awfully close to the couple's hearts.

Mirabelle still lived at home, not every night, as it was too far to travel on a daily basis, but much to the delight of her Papa, she shared an apartment in Oxford with Teddy, which helped stop the tongues from wagging.

Rajiv's parents had visited from India just after he had opened the hospital, and had been impressed, though the Maharajah had expressed his disappointment that his son had not returned to India, though he secretly thought this decision had a lot to do with Lord Fanshaw's daughter. When asked for clarification, his Lordship could neither deny nor confirm. The Maharajah, had merely shrugged and as they were enjoying the hospitality of his Lordship, made no further comment. His wife, the Maharani, felt no obligation to this hospitality, and voiced her disapproval in such terms, they cut their visit short and returned to India. Thankfully, Rajiv's father did nothing to stop his son from continuing his work at the hospital.

So with two out of three of his children settled, Lord Fanshaw was content, especially when in eighteen fifty-eight he had received a communication that not only had Joseph settled into Army life, he had gained the rank of an officer, and sent out to India to serve.

Relieved that Joseph had also settled down, it was a blow when eighteen months later, news reached him that Joseph had suffered a bad accident, breaking both legs. When his feet became gangrenous, the result was that both legs had to be amputated beneath the knees.

It was a bitter blow, one that frightened Lord Fanshaw, certain that this would surely throw his son spiralling down into a depression that would end in more disruptive behaviour. Luckily for Joseph, he was saved, and his saviour came in the form of a young English woman he had met in Delhi who helped nurse him. She had agreed to return to England with him, to continue to care for him.

With Joseph on his way home, Henry-Carmichael had to rethink his plans. When he'd sent Joseph away to join the Army, Henry had removed his eldest son as heir to the Estate, but now, he had little choice but to reverse his decision. With Joseph returning, he would need a job to do, so it would be obvious, the running of the estate should go to him when his father retired or passed away, providing he proved he would make a good and fair Lord of the manor.

How Teddy would take this, having been told the title would go to him, goodness only knew. The time had come to talk to him.

With the weekend looming, Lord Fanshaw knew he would have to talk things over with Teddy, and as Mirabelle was coming with him, he thought that a family conference would be in order. However, when they arrived on that Friday evening, he was surprised they were accompanied by Rajiv.

Over dinner, Henry-Carmichael told them about Joseph's expected arrival and more importantly, his injuries. Raj was extremely interested and asked if he would be allowed to see if there was any way he might help Joseph. Henry-Carmichael was pleased, but unsure of Joseph's attitude and said he would mention it.

He said he would need to talk to Mirabelle and Teddy about the changes that would have to made, but that it could wait until the morning as he didn't want to spoil their evening and would rather hear news of Rajiv's hospital and Teddy's life in the law office.

When they all retired that evening Henry-Carmichael suggested they meet in his office at eleven the following morning and have their discussion over coffee.

He was surprised therefore, when the others made their way upstairs, Rajiv hung back, and catching his Lordship by the arm, asked if he might speak with him in private the following morning and suggesting a ten-thirty meeting. Henry-Carmichael was intrigued, and said the arrangement was fine by him. The two men parted, saying goodnight and Lord Fanshaw deep in thought as to what on earth Rajiv had in mind.

Lord Fanshaw was already in his office by the time Teddy, Mirabelle and Rajiv came down to breakfast.

Over breakfast, Teddy asked what if anything Raj might be able to do to help Joseph's injuries.

'Well, until I meet him, I cannot be specific, but I would like to think that something can be done. Unlike yourself Teddy, Joseph as lost his legs below the knee, whereas you still have your legs, and although you suffer from muscle wastage, with the help of the leg irons and walking sticks, you are able to walk. But I would like to include you in my ideas when the time comes as I think you could be a great deal of help and encouragement to your brother.'

Teddy nodded, thoughtfully. 'Interesting. And yes, I'd be pleased to offer whatever help you think I can give. Let's hope my brother has a better attitude than when I last saw him.'

'Well, if you'll excuse me, I asked to meet with your Father at ten-thirty.' As he left the table, he put his hands on Mirabelle's' shoulders and bent to kiss her head. She rewarded him with a smile and patting his hands said quietly. 'Good luck.'

Teddy was intrigued and when the door closed quietly behind Raj, said .'So what was that all about little sister?'

Mirabelle replied laughing. 'Wouldn't you like to know brother. Well you will just have to wait, More coffee Teddy dearest?' she asked teasing him.

Well, whatever was going on, Mirabelle looked happy, and that was all that mattered.

The knock on the door was light and Lord Fanshaw almost missed it. 'Come in. Please Raj, take a seat. What can I do for you?'

'Well Sir, I have given this a lot of thought and I didn't want to do anything about it until I had time to speak to my parents. I knew they wouldn't be pleased, especially my Maa, sorry Mother. My Baap, sorry Father, is a lot more enlightened.....'

Henry-Carmichael glanced at his pocket watch, he was conscious that Mirabelle and Teddy would shortly be arriving for their meeting. 'I don't want to hurry you Raj, but could you come to the point.'

'I'm sorry Sir, the thing is, as you know Mirabelle and I have been firm friends, and working together has brought us closer. To the point where.....well I love your daughter, I love Mirabelle and I wonder Sir if you would allow me to ask for her hand, I would like to marry Mirabelle Lord Fanshaw.'

'Yes, I got that.' So many thoughts were whizzing through his mind. What would society make of
this union, and did it really matter? What were the facts? He was a Doctor, from a different country with a different religion, what if he wanted to return to India one day....... As if reading his thoughts Rajiv said.

'If you are worried about me wanting to return to India, you need have no fear. My life is here, especially as I have the hospital and hopefully, with your blessing, Mirabelle.' Henry-Carmichael nodded, taking it all in. A knock came on his door and Mirabelle burst in.

'Papa! Have you said yes?' she looked from her father to Rajiv. 'Oh please Papa, you must say yes.' and running to be at Rajiv's' side, she slipped her hand into his.

From the look they exchanged left Henry-Carmichael in no doubt they loved each other, and if a couple could work together and share their lives despite coming from such different cultures, who was he to deny them.

'You have my blessing.' he replied, smiling

When Teddy entered the study, he was surprised at all the excited voices but was soon informed the reason why. Congratulating them, he gave his sister a warm hug and shook hands with Raj, slapping him playfully on the back. 'It's good to know we'll have a doctor in the family, no more doctors bills for us.' He joked.

Rajiv took his leave good naturedly, so that Lord Fanshaw could discuss the homecoming of Joseph. When they considered the details of Joseph's injuries, both Teddy and Mirabelle were concerned, but agreed that if Joseph was willing, he should be reinstated to take over the Estate on their father's passing or when he retired.

Depending on his health, Joseph could set about learning how things were done as soon as possible, as they all agreed, they didn't want Joseph to become despondent. When they were told Joseph was returning with a young English lady, who had been nursing him in India and intended to continue doing so in Wynchampton, they were intrigued and impressed.

As soon as the meeting was over, Teddy said he was going for a ride, and went swiftly out to the stables where one of the grooms saddled up a horse for him.

He took a gentle ride to the village, he was in no hurry, but Mirabelle and Raj's announcement had made up his mind. If they were brave enough to defy convention and marry, why shouldn't he.

Eilish would still be at work and wouldn't return until the evening, but on this occasion, it wasn't Eilish he wanted to see, but her mother.

Sliding from his horse, he took his sticks and made his way awkwardly up the garden path. Shelagh was surprised to see him, knowing that her daughter wouldn't be home for several hours, but she welcomed him anyway. Opening the door, she smiled. 'Hello Teddy, and how are you?'

'I'm fine Mrs McGovern and you?'

'I'm well. You do know Eilish won't be home for some time yet.'

'Yes I know. As a matter of fact it was you I wanted to speak too.'

'Oh? Well you'd better take a seat. Can I get you anything? tea, a cold drink perhaps?'

'Tea would be lovely, but perhaps you'd better hear what I have come to say, or ask, before you make me too welcome.' He laughed a little self-consciously.

'Ooh?' Shelagh seated herself. 'Go on.' she said smiling, for surely young Teddy could not have anything to say that could cause her anguish, at least she hoped not, as she had come to love him, right or wrongly, like a son.

'Mrs McGovern, as you know, Eilish and I have been walking out, having been friends for an exceptionally long time. To be honest, my feelings for her have been a great deal stronger than I have ever let on, though I think she has guessed and can reciprocate. My delay in coming to you, has been two-fold. One, I knew to be fair to both of us, I had to be absolutely sure of those feelings, and to give Eilish time to consider the consequences of such feelings, and two, and I hope you will not be offended by this confession, that my decision would not upset my Father.'

Shelagh was amused. Teddy could be so serious at times, but to be fair, what she thought he was about to ask had to be seriously considered, and for that she was grateful. In answer, she inclined her head as if in agreement with him, which of course she was.

'So I have come here today, to ask you dear Mrs McGovern, if you would give your permission for me to ask Eilish if she would do me the honour of accepting a proposal of marriage from me, and to ask your permission for me to make that proposal?'

'Well! Teddy, that was some speech.' Shelagh was quiet for a moment, mulling over what he'd said and trying to work out what had happened to bring him so suddenly to her door. 'You say you had been waiting, as you didn't want to upset your Father? Have you spoken to him?'

Teddy smiled. 'No, but today, I am pleased to say my sister Mirabelle, has accepted the hand of Doctor Patel, and my Father has given them his blessing. From this, I know he will see no objection to me asking for Eilish's hand. Also, you may know, my brother Joseph is returning from India. Sadly, he has been gravely injured, though I understand is in good spirits, apparently all down to a young English lady who has devoted herself to his recovery and will be continuing to be by his side.'

'Well that is good news, not about his accident of course, but that he has found such a brave young woman. And as for your request to me, why of course you have me permission, and I would be delighted to have you as a son-in-law. I can think of no-one better.' Shelagh was beaming, if only Cormac could have been here, he would have been so proud of his daughter, and how sad she would be on her daughter's wedding day.

'I wonder if you would all come to Sunday lunch tomorrow, only not a word to Eilish.' Teddy said.

'That would be nice. But are you sure? After all you haven't discussed this invitation with your father' Shelagh replied hesitatingly, there was also the question of Joseph. How did she feel about her daughter entering the family of the fiend who'd attacked her daughter? And what about Eilish? She felt a cold shiver as the memory of that day flooded back.

Teddy obviously detected none of Shelagh's hesitancy. 'Good. I will send a carriage for you at eleven.' As he left, Teddy took her hands in his and leaning forward kissed her gently on both cheeks. 'Thank you Mother to be. And I promise, I will give your daughter every happiness I can for the rest of our lives.'

'I'm sure you will. 'She said smiling, but when he'd gone, she sat down heavily wondering if this future alliance could really work.

On his return to The Hall, Teddy went in search of his father. 'Stanley, have you seen his Lordship?' he asked.

'I believe he went out with Mr McGregor Sir.'

Teddy went out by way of the kitchen as he wanted to give cook a message. The smell of fresh baking assailed his nostrils and just as he'd done when a little boy, he picked a biscuit off the tray and laughing said. 'Wow! That's hot, but I had to check it Cookie.' he laughed mischievously.

'Serves you right Master Teddy.' she laughed with him. 'What am I going' to do with you?' she shook her head in mock anger .

'Put me across your knee?' Teddy joked.

'Don't tempt me.' she replied.

'On a serious note, I've come to tell you there will three more for luncheon tomorrow.

'Oh? His Lordship said there would be two extra.'

Teddy frowned. 'Well, I only knew about these three guests half an hour ago, and I haven't spoken to my Father.'

'Right, so that must mean there will be nine sitting down?'

'I suppose so. I'll check with Papa and confirm with you.'

'Thank you Master Teddy.' and as he went out, he craftily scooped another biscuit and laughing, ran off.

'I saw that.' Cook called out after him, shaking her head in amusement.

Everywhere he went, no-one had seen his father, until he caught up with the land agent, McGregor. 'Oh, your Father received a telegram to say Master Joseph and his nurse were arriving this afternoon at the railway station so he's taken a carriage to meet them.' As the news sunk in, Teddy thanked him and turned away. Joseph coming home. He knew his return was immanent but today! Of all the days he could have come home, it had to be today. What should he do now? True, he hadn't spoken to Eilish or his father, but he had spoken to Eilish's mother, and he had no wish to delay his announcement further. To hell with it! he would speak to his Papa today, no matter what time it was, and God help Joseph if his behaviour was anything but pleasant. Hopefully, a few years in the Army had mellowed him, which from the reports they'd had, he was a changed man. But what if his injuries had embittered him?

As he entered the house, maids were hurrying to and fro, preparing Master Joseph's room and the adjacent one for his nurse.

Teddy went to the lounge and rang the bell to order some tea. This was brought to him and followed by Mirabelle. 'Ah tea.' She said. 'Just what I need. Poppy, be a dear would you and bring another cup.'

'Yes Miss.' Poppy said and did a little bob. Teddy smiled, even Mirabelle's attitude and the way she spoke to the servants had changed since her time in London and with Raj, he chuckled, oh what love could do! 'What are you laughing at brother dear?' she said lightly

'You sister dear. What a change there is since meeting with our dear doctor, Ah, love.......'Teddy joked and Mirabelle blushed.

'You may mock young man, but wait until it happens to you, wait until some pretty young filly captures your heart.'

'Who says it hasn't already happened.' He teased

'What! Oh Teddy really, who is she? Please, please do tell, do we know her?'

Teddy hesitated. Would his sister still be as excited when she knew who it was he intended marrying? 'I must speak to Father before I say anything else. And Mirabelle, will you do me a favour? I intend to speak later tonight, but I don't want Joseph's homecoming over shadowed, so please, can I ask you to keep this to yourself until tomorrow morning.'

'Of course Teddy dearest.' She said going over to him and giving him a hug and a kiss. 'And I hope she will make you as happy as I am. And thank you for making darling Raj so welcome. I know our union will be frowned upon by some, but I don't care. He's a good man and a wonderful doctor.......and I do love him so.' Teddy was surprised as she said these last words, to see her eyes brimming with tears. Going to her. He hugged her.

'And I admire and support you both. I think it is right, one should marry for love and for nothing else.'

An hour later, they heard their fathers carriage arrive. Stanley was first at the door with footman rushing to the carriage to help everyone alight and to start bringing in trunks and luggage. Teddy and Mirabelle held their breath as Raj ran up the stairs to greet them and tell them that Joseph, although tired from his journey, was in good spirits and had been touched that he, Raj had accompanied their father to meet and help him.

They both relaxed on hearing this. 'And what of his nurse?' Mirabelle whispered.

'She's a delight.' Raj whispered back 'And obviously devoted to your brother. She wasn't a real nurse as such but took to looking after Joseph as an extra pair of hands. Since then I believe, an affection has grown between them. They certainly seem very fond of each other.'

'Well, well, well.' Mirabelle murmured. 'Love certainly does seem to be in the air. Is it a disease do you think Doctor?' she laughed slipping an arm through his.

'Well if it is I think it's a good one and we don't need to cure it.'
Teddy went to greet Joseph and welcome his companion who they now knew was called Emily, Mirabelle followed suit.

After a quick catch-up Joseph asked if everyone would excuse him, as after his long journey he felt like a rest but looked forward to seeing everyone later at dinner.

With Joseph and Emily resting, Mirabelle and Rajiv in the sitting room reading, Teddy took the opportunity to speak with his father, who gone to his study. 'Father, I'm sorry to trouble you, but there is something I need to speak with you about.'

'Oh? Is there a problem?' he asked Teddy, looking concerned.

'No, not a problem...it's just that, Oh dear, I know you have a lot to think about with Joseph coming home, and Mirabelle's announcement, but the thing is.....I have spoken to Mrs McGovern this day, so I cannot delay speaking to you regarding my visit to her.'

'My goodness me, whatever is it Teddy? Please, sit down and tell me what troubles you?'

Teddy smiled at his father's concern. 'No trouble Papa, only good things, well I think it's good and so does Mrs McGovern.' He took a deep breath and plunged on . 'Father, I have asked Mrs McGovern for permission to ask Eilish to marry me and she has given her consent.'

The smile that appeared in his father's face grew bigger until he was laughing and tears sprung to his eyes. Getting up he hugged his youngest son. 'Well done! My son, well done. And have you spoken to the young lady yet?'

'No not yet, though I have taken the liberty to invite the family to luncheon tomorrow, with the intention of asking Eilish on her arrival, and hopefully if she says yes, to announce it over our meal.'

'I think it's a wonderful idea, what a celebration we will have, the announcement of not one but two engagements and Joseph's home coming. I cannot see the young lady refusing you, after all, we all know you have been walking out for some time. I'm very pleased for you.' Henry-Carmichael chuckled. 'Oh dear, I thought Mirabelle's announcement would raise eyebrows, and now your announcement! Well why not, it is how it should be. Love is love, and class, colour nor religion should have any say in the matter.' Henry-Carmichael was ecstatic. He now knew that two of his children had paved the way for making his dream come true.

They gathered in the lounge for pre-dinner drinks and listened to Joseph's tales of army life. He skirted around the event that lead to his injuries, which he acknowledged would have a life changing effect on his future, but as he pointed out, these tragedies happened and could also come with positives. Henry-Carmichael was proud when Joseph went onto explain what he meant. They were the experiences and what he'd learnt in the few years he'd spent in the Army, the fact his life had been spared, and the fact he had a loving family to come back too, and a future, learning how to take care of the Estate, and improve on it in the years to come. And finally, and at this point he looked at Emily and holding out his hand to her, which she took, told of his meeting with this wonderful young woman, who was able to look beyond his disability, something that resonated with Teddy.

After dinner, Henry-Carmichael announced the engagement of his daughter, Mirabelle, to Doctor Rajiv Patel. There was loud applause from Joseph and Emily and Henry sent for champagne and asking for Stanley, to inform the servants of the news and ask them to enjoy a drink on their behalf. The butler's slight look of disdain did not go unnoticed by his Lordship, who though angry, chose to ignore it as he wanted nothing to take away the happiness that everyone else round the table, was enjoying. Wait until he hears tomorrow's news, Henry thought.

Eilish was surprised when she arrived home that Saturday evening, to be told that they had all been invited to Sunday luncheon at The Hall. Eamon pulled a face as being his day off, he'd wanted to spend it fishing, but when his mother reminded him of cooks excellent cooking, he brightened up. 'What's it in aide of do you think?' Eilish asked her mother. Shelagh shrugged and said vaguely. 'Possibly to welcome Joseph home.'

At the mention of Joseph's name, Eilish felt cold. How could her mother possibly think lunch would be a good idea, had she'd forgotten what had happened all those years ago, because Eilish hadn't. 'But Mammy, why on earth should I want to welcome him home?'

Shelagh knew this question would arise, but if Eilish was to marry Teddy, she would inevitably have to mix with Joseph. She had to be careful how she answered her daughter and not give the game away. 'The invitation came from Teddy, and it's not really to welcome Joseph, who I understand is a changed young man, but to congratulate Mirabelle and Doctor Patel.'

'Oh? What about them?' Eilish asked in surprise.

'They are to be married!'

'What! Oh my goodness! How did his Lordship take that?'

'Highly delighted so I understand. I think his Lordship is very forward thinking, and let's face it, Doctor Patel has shown his dedication to his chosen career, using his own money to build the hospital, and for never turning away those who cannot afford treatment. And as for Mirabelle, who'd have thought she would be so involved with looking after the sick and poor. Her time in London at that convent certainly paid off. It seems the same can be said for Joseph's time spent in the army. Perhaps it's time to put the past to bed?' She finished, crossing her fingers behind her back.

Eilish made no reply to this and Eamon also kept quiet. All he wanted to do was thrash the fellow, but at the time he'd been too young to take him on, and now Joseph was disabled, so it wouldn't be a fair contest. Coupled with that, he knew his sister was to all intense and purposes, walking out with Teddy. As to whether anything would come of that, only time would tell, but let's face it, if Mirabelle was marrying a brown fellow, doctor or no doctor, anything was possible.

On Sunday after church, the McGovern family sat waiting for the carriage to collect them as promised. On the dot of eleven, the carriage arrived and Teddy got down and today, with the aid of his crutches, walked down the path to greet them. The groom turned the carriage around and stepped down to help the ladies aboard.

On the Way to The Hall, they chatted amiably about things in general, but when they arrived, and were greeted on the doorstep by Henry-Carmichael and Mirabelle, Teddy asked to be excused as he wished to show Eilish something in the garden. A small smile was exchanged between Henry and Shelagh but went unnoticed by Eamon. Mirabelle felt a little uneasy as she put two and two together, and hoped that the history that lay between them, wouldn't put Eilish off.

As they walked, Teddy, was silent, thoughtful. Looking up at him, Eilish asked. 'What's going on?' Teddy smiled, teasing.

'What makes you think something is going on?'

'Well, I arrive home last evening, you don't come over as you usually do, though that could have been because your brother came home, and then Mammy tells me we are invited to have luncheon with your family today, though of course that could be to celebrate your sister and Doctor Petal's engagement, but something tells me there is something else going on. Even my Mammy seems to be acting strangely.' They had reached the stone circular paving, surrounded by roses, stone benches and a beautiful stone statue of a lady standing in the centre.

'I think this is one of the prettiest parts of the garden.' Teddy

suddenly said, gently pressing her down on one of the benches.

Eilish looked around, smiling and nodding in agreement. Suddenly, Teddy sat down beside her, taking hold of her hand with an urgency that startled her.

'Dearest, darling Eilish, If I was able, I would go down on one knee, but because of these.' He pointed to his withered legs. 'I am unable. So please say yes when I ask you, will you do me the honour of becoming my wife?' There! It was out.

It took a while for his words to sink in as Eilish just stared at him. Thinking for one minute he'd misunderstood the strength of their friendship, his eager anticipation, began to disappear.

'Oh Eilish, my love, have I got it wrong?' he asked in dismay.

Grasping both his hands and bringing them up to her lips to kiss them, Eilish looked into his eyes. Dare he hope those were tears of happiness in her eyes.

'Teddy, my darling Teddy, you really want me for your wife?'

'Yes, yes of course. Don't you know that since you came into my life as a young girl, I've always wanted to be close to you, first as a friend, but over the last couple of years, I've always known there could be no other whom I'd want to spend the rest of my life with. So Eilish, please, put me out of my misery, will you, will you take me? Withered legs as well?' he laughed at himself.

'Teddy, I have always been proud to call you my friend and admired you for not only being so brave about that terrible illness that struck you down, but how you overcame all the difficulties, and never whingeing or feeling sorry for yourself. I would be honoured to marry you. I know I will be the happiest woman alive and I promise to make you the happiest husband in the world.'

'So it's a yes?' He said laughing and her reply was to throw her arms around him and hug him tight, saying. 'Yes, yes, yes!

In the house, Joseph was worried that Teddy and Eilish were taking their time to join the rest of the family, and wondered if Eilish was taking some persuading because she didn't want to face him after what had happened all those years ago. He felt so ashamed and could not speak of it, so when Mirabelle clapped her hands with glee, he looked up. 'What are you so excited about?' he asked. Mirabelle glanced around the rest of the company assembled.

'Mirabelle........' her father warned.

Something was going on, and Joseph had no idea, neither did Eamon. The only people who knew the reason for Teddy and Eilish' delayed appearance, were the parents, Mirabelle and Raj could only guess, but

Henry-Carmichael was determined not to steel their thunder. Just then, he heard excited voices coming through the hall, the door to the sitting room burst open and in walked two extremely excited young people. 'She said yes!' Teddy cried and Eilish giggled as they raised their clasped hands into the air.

All hell let loose. Both parents and Mirabelle dashed forward to embrace and congratulate the couple, and in doing so, it dawned on Eamon, Joseph and Emily, that this announcement had been what everyone else had been waiting for.

After that, champagne bottles were opened for the second time that weekend, and the two young brides to be were soon discussing dresses, flowers and all things wedding.

Below stairs, Harold Stanley was once again informing the rest of the servants that Master Teddy was to be married, an announcement that thrilled them all until he put a damper on it when he muttered, 'To a servant girl, and an Irish one at that. What is the world coming too?' He was so disgusted, he refused to drink a toast to the happy couple, despite being told by his Lordship, to offer this to all the servants.

Luncheon eventually was served late and cook grumbled.

'Well if it's cold that's their fault, what with all these jollities going on!' Had it been stone cold, it was doubtful anyone would have noticed such was the excitement.

Joseph was relieved that Mrs McGovern and Eamon had chosen to put the past incident aside, though Eamon was a bit frosty to start with, that was until Joseph cleverly asked about his work with the blacksmith and the apprenticeship he'd undergone. Eamon, who was so absorbed with the work, he soon forgot to be hostile, and spoke animatedly about it.

When they finished eating, Henry-Carmichael suggested they took coffee and liquors in the sitting room, where there was a fire. Looking around, he thought how nice the two families had seemed to get together. How interesting it was that the different cultures, religions, and classes, could all share a meal and converse with each other so easily. If only so-called society could recognise the value of opening one's eyes.

Raj was talking to Emily and Teddy, Joseph was deep in conversation with Eamon, and Mirabelle, Eilish and Shelagh were obviously talking weddings.

'Papa, Papa?' Mirabelle was talking to him and he hadn't realised.

'Sorry Mirabelle, I was deep in thought.' He said smiling.

'Mm, probably thinking how much this is all going to cost.' She teased him.

'Not at all, not at all.'

'Well, we've got a surprise for you. We've been talking, Eilish and I, and Shelagh, Mrs McGovern said I was to call her Shelagh as we're soon to be family, the three of us think it would be lovely to have a double wedding! There, what do you think of that? Oh, and we'd like it to be a Christmas wedding.'

At that, both Teddy and Raj stopped talking and spun round looking first at their betrothed and then at each other.

'Well, why wait? We've all known each other for so long and Eilish and myself want a quiet affair, after all, Eilish only has her Mama and her brother, and we have our family around us and I doubt there will be many from our social circle will be burning to attend such eyebrow raising matrimonial. Also Papa, and I hope you will understand, but Raj and I will be having a civil ceremony because of his religion, but afterwards, we'd like a blessing in our estate chapel. This will follow on immediately after Eilish and Teddy's service. Then we can all come back here for the wedding breakfast.' There was silence for a minute, then her father burst out laughing. Turning to the bridegrooms in question. 'Well gentlemen, what say you?'

Teddy looked amused at Raj, who shrugged good naturedly.

'Why not.' They agreed in unison.

And so it was, that by the end of the evening, having had a light supper together, plans for the two weddings, to take place on Saturday the fifteenth of December were made.

The two young brides made plans about bridesmaids, Eilish said she would ask the seamstresses at Mrs Wrights' Emporium if she would design the wedding gowns, and Mirabelle said she would speak to cook first thing in the morning about making two wedding cakes.

Mirabelle then suggested, after asking her Papa's permission, that they have a private wedding breakfast, just family, then in the evening a buffet party, throwing the doors open at The Hall, for any of the servants, local villages and other friends and colleagues of Raj's and Teddy's to join them. At that point we could also invite some of local society.' She added mischievously. 'It would be an education for them to rub shoulders with others.'

It was late when Teddy asked the coachman to ready a carriage to take Eilish and her Mama and brother home, saying that he, Teddy would drive them. Doctor Patel's carriage was also brought to him and Teddy, who shared an apartment in Oxford with his sister, told Raj he would bring Mirabelle to the hospital in the morning. Raj suggested that Mirabelle might like to have the day off, but she refused saying that no, she knew there was little enough servants, and she had, had the weekend off.

When he helped Eilish down from the carriage at home, Teddy said he would meet her at lunchtime the following day and take her to buy her ring.

Eilish could hardly contain her excitement the next morning at work. She decided to say nothing until after Teddy had placed the ring on her finger. When she thought of this she sobered slightly, realising that once she was married, she would no longer be able to work at Mrs Wrights Emporium.

The ring they chose was a pale blue topaz, surrounded by an oval of diamonds, 'To match your eyes.' Teddy told her. 'And that reminds me. I have been looking at possible properties for us, I hoped you wouldn't mind living in town.'

'No, of course not. But are we to have a house of our own?' Eilish was surprised knowing Teddy shared an apartment with Mirabelle, she assumed she would move in when Mirabelle moved out.

'Of course my dear. I have been looking at some nice little villas, not far from town, within walking distance for me to get to work, and with a nice little garden for you to sit in on sunny days.'

'Oh Teddy, I never dreamed.......that sounds wonderful.'

Rajiv had already given Mirabelle her ring at the weekend as they had their engagement announcement all arranged. Hers was a ruby, surrounded by diamonds and Mirabelle had been proudly showing it off all morning, though she was sensible enough to remove it when working.

Rajiv had summoned architects, recommended by Teddy, to draw up plans for a house to be built within the hospital grounds, but with winter coming on, he told Mirabelle that he might have to move into the apartment she currently shared with her brother, until their house could be built.

CHAPTER 14

For the next two months, everyone seemed to be permanently running to keep up with themselves with arrangements for the two weddings.

Mirabelle and Eilish had meetings with the designer at Mrs Wrights' Emporium, with her permission, and materials and designs had been chosen and fittings arranged. Veils, headdresses, shoes and gloves followed, and a going away outfit for Eilish who, to her surprise, was to be taken on honeymoon. Mirabelle, Raj promised, was to be taken to India to visit his family in April, when he could arrange cover for the hospital.

A florist was called in to make bouquets and decorate the private chapel and the ballroom at Wynchampton Hall, which had not been used for years. This led to a cleaning and painting session, much to the annoyance of the butler, who thought all the fuss being made for these two weddings was over the top, considering who the groom of one was and the bride of another. Though he was careful not to be too vocal in front of the servants, whom, to his disgust, seem to think it was all wonderful.

Lord Fanshaw was also enjoying himself and delighted at being able to see more of Shelagh as what better excuse than the need to discuss wedding arrangements. Even more surprising, was Josephs' eagerness to learn about the running of the estate. He now met regularly with his father and the Estate Manager, Duncan McGregor, who reported to his Lordship that the "Wee Laddie" was learning fast and becoming a pleasure to work with.

Joseph worked each morning on his physical exercises with Emily, these had been advised by Raj, after long consultations with Joseph and

Emily. There was also talk of some special equipment, similar to Teddy's leg irons, with the idea that with the help of crutches, Joseph may one day, be able to get out of his wheelchair from time to time. Throughout all of these discussions, Joseph seemed to take in his stride, accepting that all this was experimental, and would take time.

Emily was also taking an interest in the running of the Estate, acting almost like a secretary. The more he saw of this young woman, the more Lord Fanshaw liked her. She was extremely easy to talk too, very sensible and seemed genuinely fond of Joseph. He wondered if their relationship would come to the same fruition that his other son and daughter's had or was that just wishful thinking.

As cook beat butter and sugar together and spooned in dollops of the fruit and nut mixture, liberally laced with brandy, into two three tier cake tins, the other kitchen servants wrote out lists and food orders to be placed, and jobs to be done before the big day.

Lord Fanshaw made a visit to the cellar, much to the butler's annoyance, to take stock of the wines and spirits, and more lists were created and orders placed with the wine merchant.

Instructions for the best porcelain to be washed and polished as well as the gold edged cutlery and cut-glass crystal glasses.

Invitations were sent out, most accepted, though one or two refusals had been received. Only a couple dared have the affront, to inform his Lordship of the real reason from distancing themselves from such nuptials. His Lordship crossed those off the list of guests and said nothing to the engaged couples.

The Saturday before her wedding, Eilish said a tearful thank you to Mr and Mrs Wright for the happy time she'd spent in their employ. A send-off had been arranged in their private apartment above the shop, to which all the servants had been invited. A buffet laid on with champagne, and the servants having had a collection, had bought Eilish and Teddy a beautiful set of crisp white bedding sheets and pillowcases, all edged delicately with embroidery anglaise.

Mr and Mrs Wrights' gift for them was to come into the Emporium and choose a silk Chinese rug for their new home.

Teddy had taken Eilish to view a lovely villa, and as the purchase was going through, they would be able to move in on their return from their

Shelagh, and Ruth, who'd joined them, stood back looking at Eilish. Tears sprang to their eyes as they looked at Eilish in her gown. She looked so beautiful. 'But it's the same as Mirabelle's.' Shelagh gasped in astonishment. Eilish laughed at her mother's surprise and hoped she wouldn't be disappointed.

'It was Mirabelle's' idea, she thought we'd look good dressed the same.'
'Really?'

Shelagh and Ruth stared in wonderment. The white silk gown had a huge crinoline skirt, down which lay several white lace frills adorned with tiny white satin bows. The veil, like Mirabelle's, was made of the same white lace. Although Mirabelle had been unable to have her marriage in the little chapel in the grounds of her home, she was determined to dress as any bride of her standing.

When Eilish and Mirabelle descended the grand staircase at The Hall, everyone, including the servants, who'd gathered to watch, gasped.

'Oh don't they make a picture?' Cook declared, and Eilish smiled and laughed at her one-time adversary, who was about to become her sister-in-law, and over the previous few weeks, had definitely become a friend, who'd have thought it?

With Eamon, Teddy's best man, and Teddy already at the Estate chapel, Henry-Carmichael held out his arm to Eilish, as with no father to give her away, Henry had stepped in. 'Come along everybody, you should all be making your way to the chapel.' As everyone started to rush about, Henry, turned to his daughter and Rajiv, saying. ' As soon as the marriage service is over, I will come and take you up to the alter for the blessing. At least I'll be able to do that much for my daughter.'

'Thank you Papa.' Mirabelle replied and Raj inclined his head smiling. There was no doubt, Henry told himself, he'd never seen his daughter so radiantly happy.

By the time the wedding party arrived, those that could find a seat had done so, but for the rest it, was standing room only. The villagers and servants were to the back, and in the front pews, Shelagh, Joseph and Emily sat, leaving room for Henry and Eamon.

To the side of the alter, were two red velvet throne like seats where Rajiv and his new wife Mirabelle had discretely seated themselves.

Mirabelle's entrance hadn't been ignored and much to her delight, she heard many "Oooh and Ahhs" and "Oh doesn't she look beautiful," "Like a fairy Princess".

The chapel looked stunning, decorated with foliage of different shades of green and variegated with creamy white to pale yellow. All this was interspersed with white blooms and large bows of white ribbon. Both brides and Eilish's maid of honour, carried bouquets of similar floral arrangements.

As the organist struck up, everyone stood, and Teddy couldn't help turning to have a sneaky peep at his bride. At the sight of her, he nearly broke down, she looked so beautiful. Not for the first time did he thank his lucky stars for having the father he had, who accepted, class had no place where love was concerned.

As they made their way down towards the alter, Eilish nervously looked about her. At first she only saw the servants from The Hall and many of the villagers, farmers and other workers on the Estate, this made her smile. To think that they were obviously here to support her and Teddy, although she knew that Teddy was very dear to them. She was surprised to see so many that, from their attire, appeared to be local gentry, some of whom she recognised. On second thoughts, they were probably here as acquaintance of Mirabelle and her family, or even maybe patients of the Doctor's practice in Oxford. In the second of the front pews sat three nuns, and Eilish thought how nice it was that they had come from London, for surely these must be three of the Nuns from the convent where Mirabelle had stayed.

Lord Fanshaw came to a halt. They had arrived at the altar. As she turned to hand her bouquet to Ruth, she was aware of Teddy's eyes on her, his tender smile as she stood beside him.

The marriage service seem to go through in a flash, their responses as if in a dream. Prayers were said, hymns were sung and suddenly she heard the vicar say. 'I now pronounce you man and wife.' Turning towards each other, Teddy held her hands, beaming with pride. As they walked towards the vestry for the signing of the register, Eilish couldn't believe it was all over, it had all seemed like a dream. But it was no dream as Teddy whispered in her ear. 'You are all mine now Mrs Fanshaw.'

DESSERT
Apple Charlotte
Queen Cake
Madeira Jelly
Trifle
Ice Creams
Cheese with Nuts & Grapes

FOR THE TOAST
WEDDING CAKE & CHAMPAGNE

The wedding breakfast had begun. First there was a flurry of servants and waiters some of which neither Mirabelle nor Eilish had ever seen before.

With each course, a different wine was served. Eilish, who had only ever tasted a little port wine at Christmas, looked at Teddy for guidance. 'What is it my love?'

'The wine Teddy, I've never had wine at least not like this.'

'Would you like to try some?'

'I don't think so.' She said unsure of herself but not wanting to appear ignorant. 'Would it be bad manners to ask for some barley water?'

'Of course not. Today, you and Mirabelle are the most important people here, so your wish is my command.' he whispered, teasing her and waving to attract the attention of one of the footman. 'My wife,' he said smiling at Eilish who blushed. 'Would like a glass of barley water, could you bring a jug as some of the other ladies might like some also.'

By pacing herself and only accepting small portions, Eilish was able to make her way through the menu.

As the last of the dessert dishes were removed, Henry-Carmichael stood to make a speech thanking everyone for attending, and welcoming Doctor Rajiv Patel and Eilish to the family.

At last, both brides and grooms were given large knives and they stood, pointing the tip of the knife on each cake, and with a gentle push, the knives pierced the cakes amid clapping and cheers. These were then whipped away to the kitchen to be expertly cut into small pieces to be handed round with a glass of champagne.

At the end of the meal, the guests dispersed, some of the gentlemen went with Henry-Carmichael to take a brandy and cigars, the ladies to rest.

The evening guests, began to arrive just before eight, when they were joined by those who'd attended the earlier wedding ceremony.
Upstairs, Mirabelle was eager to make her entrance with her new husband, Eilish, having found the whole day, though exciting, also overwhelming, took a deep breath and with her arm through Teddy's, followed Mirabelle and Raj down the stairs to make their entrance into the ballroom, where once again, great cheers and lots of handclapping, welcomed them.
The dancing commenced with both brides and grooms taking the floor, after which the guests joined them.
Below stairs, it was a relaxed, yet party atmosphere, except for the butler Harold Stanley, who still felt it beneath him to have to welcome a brown man, and a former Irish maid, into the family.
As soon as the servants had finished serving the buffet, at Lord Fanshaw's insistence, they were invited to have a little party of their own below stairs.
At midnight, the guest grooms, with the help of The Hall's stable lads, readied the horses and took carriages to the front, ready for their departure. A carriage had been laid on for Shelagh and Eamon, who hugged Eilish before departing, as she and Teddy promised to call on them in the morning, when on their way to the railway station, for the first leg of their honeymoon.
Two rooms had been especially prepared as bridal suites, and everyone else retired, tired, exhausted but all agreed, it had been a wonderful day.
Downstairs, the servants set too cleaning, tidying, putting furniture back in its place, and finally crawling into their beds. Still, they knew they had done his Lordship proud.

CHAPTER 15

With the weddings over, life on the Wynchampton Estate was soon back to normal. Up at The Hall, Joseph was deep in thought. He had something particularly important on his mind, and it had been there ever since the day his siblings had got married. He needed someone to talk too, but who?

Joseph had always found it difficult to express himself, although since coming home, he'd been surprised at his family's acceptance of him. There had been a little discomfort in the atmosphere when he'd first arrived, but no recriminations or reminders of his former behaviour. At first he'd put that down to the fact that Emily had been with him and he knew his father and brother were far too well-mannered to make comment. But even Mirabelle had changed. She was like another person, and what a surprise when he'd learnt of her relationship with the Doctor! Then there was Teddy, well he'd always been a lovable fellow, and Joseph felt ashamed of the way he'd treated him when they were growing up. In fact, he was ashamed of many things, and he wasn't sure how he'd been able to face Mrs McGovern and Eilish, but neither had alluded to the dreadful obscenity he'd committed on Eilish. They'd all acted as if it had never happened.

Yet despite all this, he continued to worry about it, suffering in shame. He'd never spoken of it to Emily, frightened it would send her running for the hills. But perhaps it was time to unburden himself, after all, feeling like he did about Emily, he would have to be honest with her, especially, as he recognised that like his siblings, he too had fallen in love.

As he later waited in his father's office to discuss estate business, he smiled when he recognised the voices in the hallway.

'Ah, there you are Joseph, sorry to have kept you waiting, Emily told me you were in the office, but I got waylaid by McGregor, seems poor old Tillotson passed away three days ago and the sons are eager to take over the tenancy. Can't see a problem with that can you?'

Joseph shook his head. 'No, I went out to the farm with McGregor before Christmas and then again just after when I heard the old chap was in bed poorly, but I didn't expect him to die. Still, I suppose he was getting on. But as you say, no reason not to let the sons take over, they keep the place in good condition, and the farm certainly makes a profit.'

'True. So, how are things with you? McGregor says you're doing well, getting to grips with the running of things. Any problems?'

Suddenly, Joseph knew exactly what he had to do, he could leave it no longer, time to face up to his demons. 'Emily, would you be kind enough to go down to the kitchen and ask if we could have some coffee.'

'Of course.' Emily turned to go but was stopped by Henry-Carmichael.

'Hold on, I can ring for some.' He said.

'Em, Father, I wanted to have a talk with you.' And turning to Emily Joseph said quietly. 'Do you mind Emily?'

'No, of course not, I've got some sewing to do so I'll just pop to the kitchen first. Call me when you need me.'

'Thank you dear.' Joseph said.

'Problem?' Henry-Carmichael asked his son, Joseph shook his head.

'No Father, at least not with Emily. Not with anyone really. It's me who has the problem and it's me that has to sort it.'

'Oh?'

Joseph took a deep breath. 'The thing is, since I've come back, everyone, all of you, even the McGovern's, have been so decent. None of you have turned your backs on me, or thrown back at me my previous, despicable behaviour, which in truth, makes me feel sick with shame.' As he said this, he bent his head but not before, his father saw the tears of distress roll down his face. Suddenly his shoulders shook with grief and revulsion and his father was quick to go to his side and put his arms around him, holding him until the sobbing subsided.

There was a knock on the door, which heralded a maid bearing a tray of coffee and biscuits. As soon as she had left, Henry-Carmichael, gave his son a handkerchief, patting him gently on the back. 'I think everyone recognises, that your years in the army have changed you, made a man of you, a gentleman, and you have grown up. Took a while, but perhaps we, your Mama and I were partly to blame for that. Not disciplining you, not spending enough time with you. But that's all in the past, and the future is ahead of you, for all of us. And to be honest, I'm proud of the way you've accepted the dreadful injuries you've sustained. Many a young man would have become embittered, but you've come home, and thrown yourself into the work of the estate, with enthusiasm, that I could only have dreamed of, and making a damn fine job of it as well.'

'Thank you Father, I appreciate that. And to be honest, I'm enjoying it, something I never thought I'd say. But there is one thing. Do you think I should speak to Mrs McGovern and Eilish? Apologise?'

Henry-Carmichael was thoughtful as he poured the coffee. 'Perhaps Shelagh, but I'm not sure about Eilish. I suggest if you visit Shelagh, you might ask her advice on that one.' They drank their coffee, both mulling this over

'There is one other thing.' Joseph said

'Oh?'

'It's Emily.'

'Ahhh.' His father said knowingly. So it wasn't his imagination.

Joseph smiled, a light laugh escaped as he said. 'Is it that obvious?'

'Well......She is an attractive and attentive young lady. It's pretty obvious that she has a great fondness for you. And to come all this way from India to look after you...........well, I think that has to say something. So, what about Emily?'

'Father, I think I would like to ask her to marry me.'

'You think?'

'I know. But do you think I should tell her what a dreadful chap I had once been? I don't think there should be any secrets between a couple. And if she were to find out in the future, after we were married, I couldn't bear it if it destroyed us, but I'm scared if I tell her, she'd want nothing more to do with me.'

His father gave this dilemma some thought before he answered. 'Perhaps you should first speak with Shelagh, Mrs McGovern. Then speak with Emily. There is no need to go into details, which would be harrowing for both of you, just that you weren't always the nicest of young men, but your stint in the army, paid off.' Henry-Carmichael was pleased to see his words had a reassuring effect on his son.

Later that afternoon, he was pleased to see one of the grooms helping Joseph up onto his horse, then accompany him out of the yard, going in the direction of the village. His injuries not stopping him for riding.

Two hours later they were back and Joseph looked as if a weight had been lifted off his shoulders.

CHAPTER 16

Shelagh had been surprised when she looked out of the window that cold February day and saw Joseph and a groom ride up and stop at the gate.

Helped down from his horse, Joseph, with the aid of his groom and crutches, made their unsteady way down the frosty garden path. Shelagh swiftly opened the door to usher them in, but the groom said he would wait outside for his master. Surprisingly, Joseph told the young man he would be as quick as possible as it was very cold outside.

Shelagh offered him a hot drink, which he declined though asked if his groom could have one whilst they talked. This consideration for a servant certainly was a change in attitude Shelagh thought as she hurriedly made a drink and took it out to the groom, who was very appreciative.

'Thank you for seeing me Mrs McGovern, I will be brief as I do not wish to keep my groom waiting too long in the cold. This is so exceedingly difficult, now I'm here I do not know where to start, so I will just say what I have come to say and hope you will find it in your heart to hear me out. I have come to apologise for my despicable behaviour I metered out to your daughter all those years ago. I do not hope for your forgiveness and Eilish's although I do not deserve it, but as we are all now one family, I hope you will accept my sincere sorrow at my cowardly behaviour, and I'm wondering if I should speak with Eilish and make my apologies to her? You see Mrs McGovern, I have met a young lady whom I wish to marry, and I'm fearful that should what happened ever come to her ears, it could destroy us so I feel I must be honest with her and admit I haven't always been the nicest of young men.'

Shelagh had been standing during Joseph's speech, now she sat down with a thud. For a moment there was silence as his words of remorse swirled in her brain. What to do? How to reply? Shelagh thought over the last few months since Josephs' return, the engagement, the wedding and the recent Christmas and New Year the two families had shared. Taking a deep breath she looked him in the eye, and Joseph was surprised and relieved, when he saw there was no hostility in them.

'What you did, encouraged by Mirabelle, was a dreadful thing. But I think we all know, that over the last few years, both of you have turned your lives around and proved that you are not evil. Eilish has found love and great happiness with your brother, and Mirabelle is certainly proving herself an ideal wife and partner with Rajiv. I think we have all moved on. We have spent many happy occasions, the two families since the incident and managed to put it behind us. I think Eilish would prefer it to stay that way. I think if you feel you must say something to your intended, do not go into too much detail as this could be distressing, but confirm to her that you have made your apologies to the family concerned, and that they have accepted them and wish to close the curtain on the matter. Now go and ask for the young lady's hand with our blessing.' She finished kindly.

Joseph sat for several minutes. How could she be so calm and understanding? If Eilish turned out like her mother, his brother had a wonderful wife. Right now, he, Joseph, felt even more humbled.

'Thank you. Thank you Mrs McGovern, I don't deserve it, but I thank you from the bottom of my heart.' Joseph took his leave, and the conversation was repeated by Shelagh to Henry the following day when he called.

Joseph couldn't wait to speak to Emily on his return from his visit to Shelagh. He decided to take Shelagh's advice and not give too much information, and especially no mention of Eilish's name as that could cause serious embarrassment. As Shelagh said, the curtain needed to be closed for good.

He found Emily in the library, curled up on a sofa in front of the fire, reading a book. She looked so lovely he just hoped he wouldn't lose her.

'Emily, I must speak with you.' He said rushing in and reaching for her hands. Emily looked up, concern at his agitation.

'What on earth is it? And where have you been? I came to find you but your father said you'd gone out but he wasn't sure where.'

'Yes my love, I needed some time to think. Emily, there is something of great importance I wish to ask you, but before I do, I have to tell you something that is not pleasant. It is something that for my shame, I am to blame, and for which I deeply regret and I only hope that like the person I wronged, you too can put it behind us.'

'Good heavens Joseph, whatever is it?'

Joseph took a deep breath and went to stand by the fireplace. 'Many years ago, I was a spoilt, disrespectful, lout.' Emily gasped putting a hand to her mouth, she could hardly believe what she was hearing, this did not sound like the Joseph she knew. Joseph continued. 'I treated not only the servants with disrespect, but my brother, my Father and anyone I came into contact with. I was thrown out of schools and university, but nothing could be as degrading as the final act that had me serving in the army. I don't want to go into details, partly because of the shame but also because I do not want to distress you, but I have to confess because if I don't, it could have dire consequences for us, for our future.'

'Go on.' Emily said, though she was fearful about what she was about to hear.

'I was angry, and furious that one of the servants was not frightened of me, in fact she was disdainful of me. One afternoon, I had been drinking, I..........I caught her alone, and cornered her. She...........' Joseph shook his head as tears coursed down his face. 'Oh Emily, I.....I'm so ashamed, but the family concerned have moved on, and amazingly, having apologised, they say it was a long time ago and I was a different person and they have closed the curtain on the incident and I should do the same. But, you see Emily, I could not until I had confessed to you.'

In the grate, the logs crackled and spat in the ensuing silence. Emily, shocked and trying to digest Joseph' confession, was having difficulty. She could not take it in that he could ever have had such a cruel, violent side to him. 'And where do I come into all of this? Why is there such a need to confess to me?'

Moving back to her, Joseph sat down and grasping her hand looked beseechingly at her. 'Because dearest Emily, I love you and want you to become my wife!'

'Oh!' Emily said jumping up. The very thing she had secretly dreamt of had come true, but now, with this confession, did she really know the young captain she had fallen in love with? She was confused and frightened. 'I'm sorry Joseph, this has all come as a terrible shock to me. Please, will you allow me.....I must have some time.....Em, I must go to my room, I need to think.' Joseph watched as the love of his life fled the room.

That evening, Emily did not join them for dinner, instead she sent one of the maids to excuse her saying that Miss Emily had a headache and asked to be excused. She asked to have a light supper sent to her room. Joseph's father thought this odd but said nothing, instead he planned to see Shelagh the following day to see is she could shed any light on the situation. Joseph considered going to Emily but thought he should leave her to work things out for herself, with no pressure from him.

Upstairs, Emily hardly touched the meal she'd requested. When it came to it, she had no appetite. She went over and over what Joseph had confessed to her and somehow she just couldn't reconcile such an action with the Joseph she knew. If only she could talk to someone, but who? She certainly couldn't discuss such a matter with his Lordship, nor could she speak to any of the servants. Mirabelle and Eilish could not be approached, that would put them in a dreadful position, so who?

Then it came to her, Shelagh McGovern! Surely Mrs McGovern was as neutral as you could get, and whether she knew of the incidence or not, she'd known Joseph for many years and at least she would be able to reassure her that he wasn't really the evil bully he'd described?

Emily did not go to help Joseph ready for bed that night. She felt guilty about this but she felt she couldn't face him until she'd seen Mrs McGovern. However, the following morning she'd calmed down, and went to help him and administer the balms to his stumps and the padding he needed when wearing the false legs he wore from time to time. These, with either his crutches or sticks, helped him walk and this in turn helped him feel less like a cripple.

There was little conversation between them, but as she went to leave his room, Joseph stopped her. 'Emily...?' She turned and her heart gave a little flip as she saw the beseeching look he gave her. She smiled. 'Not now Joseph.' This said gently, kindly. 'I have to go out for a while. You will be alright with your Father?'

'Yes. Yes, we have the Tillotson brothers coming to sign the new tenancy.'

Emily nodded, and smiling again, left the room.

In the yard, Emily sought out one of the stable lads asking him to saddle up one of the horses. Slowly, Emily left the yard and headed for the village.

When Shelagh answered the knock on the door, she was surprised and a little taken aback when she saw who it was. She knew at once what this would be about but hoped with all her heart that Joseph had kept all names to himself. She knew she mustn't give the game away and acted surprised. 'Why Emily! What a surprise. What brings you here?'

'Mrs McGovern. Please, may I speak with you?'

'Of course my dear, whatever is it?'

'A long story that I cannot make head nor tail of, and I have no one else I can talk too.'

'Well come on in. Come, sit by the fire and warm yourself. Would you like a hot drink? You must be frozen.'

'Thank you, that's very kind of you.'

Whilst Emily removed her cloak and settled herself, Shelagh busied herself making two cups of hot chocolate. Then heaving a sigh, and trying to calm herself, she went back to sit down and deal with the dilemma.

By the time Emily had finished her story, Shelagh had, had time to focus, especially when it was clear that Joseph had been economical with the details. Shelagh was able to relax and give thought to the answers this lovely young woman required. There were a few minutes of silence when Emily finished, her story, whilst Shelagh was thoughtful. Smiling, she spoke at last.

'I do know about the incident.' She said gently. 'Lord Fanshaw came to see me. He was in a terrible state, blaming himself for his lack of discipline, which was unfair really, especially when there are two parents, but one shouldn't speak ill of the dead. He did the only thing he could under the circumstances. He helped the family concerned move on with their lives, and contained what could have been a terrible scandal. There is no or was, any excuse for Joseph's behaviour, but since then, he has turned over a new leaf and has become a young man of great potential especially when you consider what he has been through recently. Such injuries he sustained, could easily have turned him back into a selfish, inconsiderate person, but it hasn't, on the contrary he has accepted his fate, and returned to take on the roll he was born too. And now he has you.'

'Emily listened to all Shelagh had to say and began to see another side to the story. She decided to confide in Shelagh.

'Joseph wants to marry me.'

Shelagh nodded thoughtfully. 'And you, do you want to marry Joseph?'

Emily swallowed hard and lifted her tear-filled eyes to meet Shelagh's. 'Ye..yes. At least I thought I did, but now? Now I'm unsure. Is he not the man I thought he was?'

'I think he is exactly the young man you thought he was. This incident took place many years ago, and if you can put it behind you, you should. Well, that's my opinion, and let's face it, everyone deserves a second chance, don't you think? There is another thing. Joseph didn't have to tell you, but it was because he wanted to be honest with you, that he took the decision to confess his wrongdoing, risking losing you, which I think if he did, he would be devastated. He's a changed man and he loves you of that I have no doubt. My advice would be, look at the Joseph you first met, and remember the young man you fell in love with.'

Emily rode back to The Hall slowly, she had a lot to think about. As she rode into the yard, she saw a commotion. Stable lads, maids and McGregor were struggling and running hither and thither. As she slid off her horse, Poppy saw her and came running over. 'Oh Miss, I'm so glad you've arrived! It's Master Joseph, he's had a fall.' Emily dropped the reigns of her horse and ran swiftly towards Joseph who was laying on the ground in obvious pain but gritting his teeth trying not to make a fuss.

'Oh Emily, thank goodness!' He panted.

'Miss Emily, I'm so sorry.' McGregor was obviously worried. 'But he insisted on riding out with his false legs on and wouldn't let me help him down. He lost his grip on the saddle as he slipped down and crashed to the ground, I think I ought to call for Doctor Patel.'

'Yes I agree, Mr McGregor......'

'No, no, no.' Joseph cried out, 'I will be alright, I just need to get these things off and perhaps a gentle massage, please Emily.'

'You will do as you are told. Where is his Lordship?' Emily asked

'He's gone out.'

'Right then in that case, please send one of the grooms to ride out and ask Doctor Patel to come as soon as possible. In the meantime, can we find a door or a plank of wood and carry Master Joseph to his room.'

Half an hour later, Joseph was in his room and Emily was administering first aid and giving him a pain killing herbal mixture sent up be Cook. Now in the comfort of his bed, with the herbal mixture taking effect, Joseph took hold of Emily's hand and brought it to his lips. 'I was so worried, you'd been gone so long, I thought you'd left me.' Hot tears trickled down his face. Emily bent over kissing him lightly on his lips and drying his face.

'No my love, I will never leave you. And if you still have it in mind to make me a permanent fixture in your life, the answer is yes, and the sooner the better.'

Had he been able too, Joseph would have leapt out of bed, but the combination of the lack of legs and Cook's remedy, sleep overcame him. ...Emily remained at his side knowing she had made the right decision. As soon as she saw he was in trouble, her heart turned over. At first she thought something much worse had taken place and she'd lost him for good, that feeling of fear was too much to bear, and she vowed that she must keep him safe, the past was the past and could not be changed but must be buried.

Joseph soon recovered as Raj diagnosed sever bruising which would be cured by rest. He also ticked him off for acting so foolishly.

Confined to bed, he and Emily had plenty of time to talk and discuss their future life together.

Henry-Carmichael had paid a visit to Shelagh and was surprised when she told him about her earlier visitor, and Joseph's.

When he returned to The Hall and heard about the accident, he went immediately to his son's room only to find he was sleeping and Emily was by his side. She informed him of the details and assured him there was no harm done. The fact Emily was there, gave him hope that all was well between the young couple.

It was several days before Joseph was strong enough to resume work and at the weekend Raj and Mirabelle paid them a surprise visit. Raj checked Joseph's injuries and pronounced him well and truly on the mend and added another warning about not to take such risks again.

'I think we should announce our intentions next weekend don't you think?' Joseph whispered to Emily just before Raj and Mirabelle prepared to leave. Emily nodded in agreement.

'Hm, I wonder if you could come next Saturday evening for dinner, stay the night if possible.' Joseph asked Mirabelle and Raj looked at each other then at her father. Henry shrugged, he had no idea.

'Just thought it would be nice for all of us to see each other. Perhaps you could call and see Teddy and Eilish, ask them as well. We haven't all been together since New Year.'

'Okay, that would be nice, yes, I'm sure we can arrange cover at the hospital and hopefully Teddy and Eilish will have nothing planned.'

'Oh and could you ask Teddy to collect Mrs McGovern and Eamon, we'll invite them too.' Then turning to his father he said. 'Could you call on Mrs McGovern and ask if she and Eamon would like to join us, I'm sure they'd love the chance to see Eilish.'

Lord Fanshaw feigned ignorance of the reason there was to be a sudden dinner party, but informed Mrs Green to ask cook to lay on something special for the following Saturday evening. Also to ask for four guest rooms to be prepared as he thought in view of what he thought may be a celebration, their guests may find it more conducive to stay overnight and perhaps make a weekend of it and stay for Sunday luncheon.

When he called in the week at Shelagh's, and proffered the invite, he would not be drawn, and just laughed secretively, though Shelagh thought she knew what he was thinking, and was pleased that the young couple had taken her advice.

Joseph took Emily by carriage into Oxford two days later. There, he purchased a beautiful diamond ring. After making sure it fit, it was put into its red leather box, for him to produce on Saturday night. Their plans already made, and ready with a full announcement at the same time. Eighteen sixty-one would be their year.

Joseph threw himself back into work and dismissed McGregor's concerns at his accident, telling him it was not his fault, it was his, Joseph's for not taking extra care.

CHAPTER 17

Saturday arrived and as maids ran about preparing rooms for the overnight stay, laid up the table in the main dining room, and cook busied everyone and shouted at those who got under her feet, Harold Stanley groaned. 'Now what!'

Late afternoon, Teddy, Eilish, Shelagh and Eamon arrived. They were greeted by Emily who apologised for his Lordship and Joseph not being there, as she explained they were with the veterinary because one of the horses had been taken poorly. Eamon immediately asked if he could be excused to join them.

Since working first at The Hall and then with Joe the blacksmith, Eamon had become increasingly eager to work more with horses. Of late, his dream had been to wonder if it were possible for him to train as a vet. Was he clever enough? He knew you had to have examinations to get into university, then there was the cost. Why did everything to enable a body to better themselves always involve money? He was now getting paid a proper wage since qualifying, and as Joe said, Eamon had increased his business not only because they could take on more work, but because Eamon was a very likeable lad.

The ladies took the chance to catch up, with Emily telling them about the work that was being carried out on the dower house. Shelagh was intrigued about this and wondered just what Henry had in mind.

…When all three of the men trooped back in, Mirabelle and Rajiv had just arrived, but it was not good news that the men had about the horse. It appeared that Cinnamon, the horse, had to be put down due to a serious problem for which there was no cure. It cast a sadness over the group which worried Emily who thought they might have to delay their announcement as she did not want it to appear callous of the horse's demise. However, when she suggested this to Joseph, he decided to take his father into their confidence and ask his advice.

Henry-Carmichael was thrilled, though not all that surprised when Joseph explained the reason for this dinner party. He was especially touched when his son told him of Emily's concerns over the announcement. He smiled as he thought about the dilemma, then made the decision that Joseph was thankful for.

'I think you should go ahead and make your announcement. It's been a sad day for us, but I think your news will give us something to be happy about and let me be the first to congratulate you. Now where is the young lady concerned, perhaps you could go and get her before we all go into dinner.'

Joseph went to call Emily away from the others, and having kissed her on both cheeks, Henry-Carmichael welcomed her to the family, and thanked her for her consideration over the horse, but insisted that the announcement went ahead.

'Now Joseph, I think you and I need to go upstairs and get washed and changed before dinner. Could I ask you Emily, to ring for Stanley and ask him to organise pre dinner drinks in my absence?'

'Of course your Lordship.'

'Ah......I think Papa or Father will be more in keeping from now on.' He replied. 'About your parents? Have you spoken to them?' he asked looking at both of them.

'We both wrote to them, indicating the way things were going......I'm afraid Emily's Papa is not impressed. It seems he had in mind a young army captain, one with both his legs intact.' Joseph replied somewhat bitterly which brought Emily swiftly to his side, clutching his hand and adding to his comment.

'But it is my life and Joseph and I love each other.' She said firmly, blushing as she said it. 'And I know he will make a good husband and.......a wonderful father when the time comes.' Which added more blushes.

Joseph's father nodded, smiling and patted her on the shoulder. 'Good for you. Come now Joseph, before we are late and have to endure Cook's wrath.'

Dinner had gone down well, the excellent menu Emily and cook had chosen, together with a good selection of wines and the happy chatter of the family, now firm friends, helped to lift the mood after the days sad event.

As Henry-Carmichael requested coffee and liquors to be taken in the lounge, Joseph stood up and called for their attention. Those who'd started to stand, sat down again, and looked anxiously at Joseph. Smiling, he turned towards Emily, holding out his hand for hers. 'Everybody, please would join with me in welcoming the future Mrs Emily Fanshaw to the family.' As Emily stood, Joseph took the ring from the box and placed it on her finger.

There were gasps, excited giggles and shouts of wonderful, and congratulation The younger ones jumped up and ran to shake hands with Joseph, and kiss Emily, who was quite overcome by the family's welcome.

Shelagh glanced at Henry, smiling. 'You knew, didn't you?' he stated, grinning. 'You cunning little minx, you said nothing.' he whispered jovially. Shelagh tried to look innocent, but failed miserably as she too was laughing.

'I'm saying nothing.' She humoured him.

As everyone was busy admiring the ring and talk of a wedding already started, they missed the look that past between the two oldest persons in the room, though never too old to fall in love, the look of intimacy was not lost on Harold Stanley as he brought in the champagne, as requested earlier, And as he left the dining room, he could be heard to groan and whisper to himself. 'Whatever next!'

Downstairs in the kitchen, the servants celebrated. Emily had been taken to their hearts and considered to be the making of Master Joseph. With her as their future Mistress, they had no doubt The Hall would be in safe hands.

Later, when they'd all calmed down, discussions restarted about wedding plans and everyone was surprised when Joseph informed them that the couple had already made their plans. To everyone's surprise, it was to be a simple wedding, as Joseph explained.

'As Father knows, we have Emily's parents' consent, although they will be unable to attend due to the length and time involved with travel from

India, where her father is still serving with the army. As we have known each other for a considerable time, Emily and I feel there is no need to wait further, so we would like to marry in April, and in our chapel on the estate. We would also like a small wedding, close family only, which of course includes you, Mrs McGovern and Eamon. I would like to ask my brother Teddy to be my best man, and I think my fiancé has a request. Emily?'

Emily stood and shyly thanked everyone for their congratulations and the asked. 'I wonder if I could ask Mirabelle and Eilish if they would be my maids of honour?' Which the girls greeted with squeals of delight. Then turning towards her future father-in-law asked. 'And if you, your Lordship... Papa, would give me away?' She finished, blushing.

Henry-Carmichael stood and went to kiss his future daughter-in-law on the cheek. 'I would be most honoured my dear.'

As the young people chatted and drank, Eamon sought out Raj for advice as to whether he thought his desire to become a vet totally ridiculous, or a possibility, and if he knew how to go about it.

Shelagh turned to Henry. 'I understand you have had the Dower House, renovated?'

'Yes, to a point.'

'Is this for Joseph and Emily?'

'No. As a matter of fact, I started it last year, long before I knew anything of my children's plans. It had been on my mind for some time, and over the last few months things have all fallen into place, it seems the perfect time to complete my idea.'

'Oh? I'm intrigued.' Shelagh said. 'May I know more?'

'Not tonight my dear. But may I ask if tomorrow morning you would be kind enough to do me the honour of taking an early morning stroll with me? There is something I'd like to show you.'

The party eventually broke up, and everyone, exhausted but happy, retired to their beds, stating they wouldn't be getting up too early, all except for two who had a whispered assignation for breakfast at eight.

It was only just getting light as Shelagh tip-toed down to the breakfast room the following morning. She had been awake since just after six, mulling over the conversation she'd had with Henry the previous evening, not that he'd given her much to go on. It was a real mystery.

Henry was already at the table, though he had not started eating, preferring to await his guest. Seeing her come through the door at this early hour looking fresh, beautiful and so very happy, he wondered if he would be lucky to make this a regular morning occurrence. Shelagh smiled at him.

'Good morning Henry, did you sleep well?'

…'Indeed I did, and you my dear?'

'Yes, especially after all the excitement and the wonderful meal Cook served up, I wonder if I might thank her or do you think that would be presumptuous of me?' She neglected to admit she'd been awake since six, thinking about what this early morning meeting was about.

Henry shook his head, smiling at the use of such a big word. 'No, no, I'm sure Cook would be most gratified for the compliment.' Something she'd never had from her late Mistress Lucinda, he thought. 'Now, what can I offer you this morning?'

Shelagh leant back against the chair, patting her stomach gently. 'I don't think I can do much justice to what's been laid out, I'm still full from last night, but perhaps a little scrambled egg, toast and tea.'

'Then I think I will join you.' He said. They breakfasted together in companionable silence, and once finished, collected outdoor capes and footwear.

As they trod the frosty footpath, Shelagh looked up, commenting on the sun, straining to show itself through the cloud.

'I think it's got the promise of a nice day, even if it's to be a cold one.'

'Yes, roll on the Spring. When I decided to have the work done on the Dower House, it was April, almost a year ago. I remember looking out of one of the bedroom windows and noticing in the gardens, the first signs of Spring, daffodils and all manner of wildflowers pushing their way up through the grass.'

'Is that where we are going now?'

'It is.' and as he said this, Shelagh could see just yards away, the most beautiful, idyllic cottage. She gasped.

'Is this it?' She asked, and Henry was thrilled when he saw her eyes light up and the expression of sheer delight on her face.

'Oh Henry! It's beautiful. How long is it since it was lived in?' Shelagh asked

Henry was thoughtful. 'About.....twenty-six, twenty-seven years. My Mother came to live here just after I was married, she didn't get on with my late wife. She died not long after Joseph was born. I often wonder, had she lived would Joseph and Mirabelle have had a better start in life. My Mother was a great disciplinarian, not harsh, but strict. But sadly it wasn't to be.'

They had walked up the path, and Shelagh was looking about her, imagining the flowers she would grow if she lived here. Henry unlocked the door and held it open for her. 'It's not finished yet, I had the men just repair and get it into a habitable abode, but I thought you would be the ideal one to advise me what was needed to finish it, making it into a real home.'

Shelagh stepped inside and was mesmerised, it was huge, well to her it was.

'This is the entrance hall, there are three other reception rooms, a dining room, drawing room and sitting room. The kitchen is through here, and through there the scullery and if you open that door, it leads to the pantry. Upstairs there are four bedrooms and three bathrooms and water closets. So, what do you think? How should I finish it?'

'The furniture?'

'All left from my dear Mama. Should I dispose of it do you think?

'Oh no!' Shelagh said quickly, shocked that anyone should want to destroy such beautiful objects.

'I should like your help with the soft furnishings, advise me on colour, drapes, rugs. Perhaps a visit to Mrs Wrights Emporium in Oxford?'

'I think that an excellent idea Henry, and yes I'd love to help you.'

'Please, will you just sit for a while, although I realise it's rather cold, perhaps you would prefer to return to The Hall?'

'No, it's alright. I can sit here and imagine I'm sitting in front of a blazing log fire.'

'Shelagh, there is something of importance I wish to discuss with you.'

'Oh?'

'But first I must tell you a little of myself. My marriage was not a happy one. It was not of my making, but of an arrangement made by my father and Lucinda's. My father was a feckless man, a gambler, lazy and without any consideration for my poor Mother. Unbeknown to her, he'd gambled away, money, works of art, and finally, Wynchampton Hall. When he realised what he'd done, he threatened suicide. Luckily for him, though unluckily for me, the man he'd lost too was a man of dubious trade, though wealthy and a social climber. He would allow my father to keep The Hall, on the condition he persuaded me to accept his daughters hand in marriage, and at the same time, hand over the running and total control of the estate to me immediately. My father did not like the idea of me taking over, though he was quite happy to see me married off. The reverse of the condition was to my liking. Taking over would be a God send, marriage to Lucinda, not so inviting, but to be fair at that point I had not met her. An introduction was arranged, and she seemed a pleasant enough young woman, quiet, or so I thought, and probably just as uneasy as I was with the arrangement. But with a father like she had, probably pleased to get away. I'm ashamed to say I saw myself as something of a saviour of this young girls fate. My Mother on the other hand, did not take to her, on the contrary, she saw right through Lucinda's act, but was powerless to warn me. Without this union, we would lose Wynchampton.'

'I'm so sorry.' Shelagh said sympathetically laying a hand on his.

'I'm sure your marriage was not like mine. And I'm sure you know from talk what mine was like.' Shelagh thought back to her marriage to Cormac. 'No, my marriage was not like yours. Cormac was a wonderful husband and Daddy. We were incredibly happy, but poor. So poor Cormac couldn't see a way out, in the end he took the gamble and took what savings we had and made the journey to England. And then we struck lucky, we came across Wynchampton and you. You might not have been your wife's saviour, but you have certainly been ours.' The way she looked up at him relieved him of all his senses and before he knew what he was doing he'd taken her into his embrace and as he kissed her, properly for the first time, to his delight she returned his kisses just as passionately.

He would not wait a moment longer. 'Shelagh, will you marry me? I cannot offer you The Hall as I wish to hand over to Joseph as soon as possible, so I can live a peaceful life, enjoying the grandchildren I hope will soon be forth coming, so would you be content to live here with me?' There! he'd said it

It all happened so fast, Shelagh's head was in a whirl. What had he said? Had he really asked her to marry him?

'What did you say?' She asked incredulously.

'I said would you marry me and live in the Dower House with me? Why not throw caution to the wind, after all isn't that what all my children have done, and they are happy aren't they?'

Now Shelagh was laughing, her head thrown back laughing like a young girl. And why not. The rest of the Fanshaw family had defied society and convention, why not them.

They walked back to The Hall arm in arm but decided to keep their announcement until after Joseph and Emily's wedding.

Just before they entered home, Henry asked. 'How about a June wedding for us?'

Shelagh smiled up at him. 'A June wedding it is.' she agreed.

CHAPTER 18

Wednesday April the seventeenth eighteen sixty-one and The Hall was alive with the sound of laughter. Mirabelle had arrived the day before with Teddy and Eilish, Raj would arrive in the morning having stayed on at the hospital the previous night.

Lord Fanshaw had given instructions that only a light breakfast would be required in the morning as there was so much excitement the young ladies might be taken poorly if they had too much to eat. This was greeted with relief by cook who had enough to do with the wedding breakfast. Still at least it would be a much quieter affair than the previous ones.

His Lordship had taken out a notice in the society columns of the main newspapers, announcing Joseph and Emily's betrothal with the information it was to be a strictly family affair as Miss Emily Goodrich's family, serving in India would be unable to attend, and due to Mr Joseph's recent injuries received in action, he preferred a smaller, more private nuptial.

While the maids were called upon to help dress and arrange hair for the bride and maids of honour, Henry-Carmichael, Joseph and Teddy, took coffee and brandy in his study, relaxed they chatted about mundane things.

The chapel had been decorated the day before by some of the servants, and the Vicar and Registrar were due to arrive at The Hall at half past eleven. The service would begin at mid-day.

It was a lovely bright sunny day, and as luck would have it, the wind had dropped so it was quite warm in the sun.

The gifts the couple had received, were many, which quite surprised them. Even more surprising was that many had been arriving from India.

Both Joseph and Emily couldn't wait to open them. One of them, Emily was relieved to see, had come from her parents. She recognised the handwriting and was glad and hoped that this was proof they'd accepted her choice of husbands, after all, one day she would be Lady Fanshaw, which was probably what they'd realised, and being the social climbers they were, it had helped to change their minds towards the union.

With the Vicar, Registrar, Teddy and Joseph on their way to the chapel, Henry-Carmichael watched with a touch of sadness, as his two sons both struggled with their disabilities. They would soon be greeted by Shelagh, Eamon and Rajiv who would have gone straight to the chapel.

Looking up to the top of the stairs, he smiled at his future daughter-in-law. What a lovely young woman she was, and how lucky had all his children been, each one finding true love he was sure of that. Yet not one of the unions, he was sure would have the blessing of most of society, but he felt sure society could learn a lot from their choices.

Holding out his arm to her, Emily glided down the stairs calm and happy. The short carriage ride to the chapel gave Emily time to look around her, surprised at the many estate workers, tenant farmers and servants from The Hall, who had turned out to wave and wish her good luck. Henry-Carmichael was also pleased they had taken the trouble to pay Emily such respect, it was yet another sign that his son had chosen well, that all who'd met Emily, approved.

The music echoed sweetly round the small chapel as they made their way down the aisle. Joseph and Teddy, along with the rest of the family, turned and murmured their approval of the bride in all her finery. Behind them, Mirabelle and Eilish walked sedately, nervously trying to stifle their excitement.

The two brothers stood with the aid of their sticks throughout the service, but neither of them would give in to the pain that standing so long would be inevitable.

At last, the vicar pronounced them husband and wife and they were able to head for the registry office to sign as husband and wife. Kisses, hugs and "welcome to the family" was said many times over.

Back at The Hall, welcome drinks were handed out, before they all headed to the dining room and Emily and Joseph were thrilled at the decoration of the room. 'Well you couldn't be a bride and not have a beautiful room to have your first repast with your husband.' Mirabelle declared. Everyone took their seats, which included the vicar, registrar, organist and their three wives, Henry-Carmichael having thought these extended invitations only good manners.

The menu was not as elaborate as Mirabelle's and Eilish's' had been, yet Emily and Joseph enjoyed it every bit as much, and when it came to cutting the cake, Emily was touched at the trouble cook had obviously gone too.

Then it was time for Henry-Carmichael to officially welcome Emily to the family, after which Teddy spoke of his brother, tactfully skipping over any of his previous history. Just as they thought it was all over, and everyone should move from the table, Henry-Carmichael rapped a spoon on the table for everyone's attention. 'Before we alight, and I have you all together, I have an announcement to make.' Everyone reseated themselves looking at each other, quizzically. 'We've had a few weddings in recent months, who would have thought it, each of my children marrying in such quick succession.....' At this, a little quirky smile on his lips, his eyes lit up with humour. '........some might say defying society, even shocking it, but their chosen ones, chosen with love, what better way to choose someone to spend your life with.' Henry took a deep intake of breath. 'So following in your footsteps, I, we, have decided to follow you along the path to matrimony.' The assembled party looked from one to the other, completely mystified. Who on earth could he be talking about? All except Eamon, who because it would affect him the most, had been informed of what was to come several days before. And to his intense gratitude, Henry-Carmichael had been kindness himself, asking if Eamon would have any objection to his marrying his Mother. How could he have any objections when he saw not only the happiness in his mother's eyes, but the gratitude and respect he had for this man, for all he'd done for the family since they'd arrived in Wynchampton all those long years ago.

Keeping silent with his knowledge, he couldn't help catching his mother's eye and exchanging a secret smile. As he did so, Henry turned and took hold of Shelagh's hand. There was a gasp, and a giggle from Mirabelle as it suddenly became clear.

'I have asked and been accepted by Shelagh, that she marry me.' Around the table, they exploded with cries of happiness, congratulations and questions of "when?" Mirabelle was the first to jump up and run round the table, throwing her arms around both Shelagh and her father.

'How soon can I call you Mother?' she asked excitedly. Shelagh laughed, relieved they had all taken the news so well. Eilish was a little more calm than Mirabelle, but it was obvious by the huge grin on her face that she was delighted, in fact everyone was. But there was more to come.

'As to when, well, Shelagh and I feel that as we have known each other for many years, and given our age...' There was a lot of teasing and laughter at this, like "Poor old things" Henry laughing, held up his hand and continued. 'The wedding will be soon.' Turning to the vicar and registrar he asked, 'We thought possibly a date in June could be arranged?' Both men nodded in agreement, smiling. Well, no-one could say his Lordship wasn't progressive in his views of life, and looking round the room, who could argue with this when you saw what happiness the mixture of cultures and classes had brought.

Squeals of delight came from the ladies, and guffaws from the men. Joseph shook his head smiling and turned to Teddy, 'Pa certainly hasn't let the grass grow under his feet.'

Teddy chuckled in reply. 'Can you blame him?'

'And lastly, and I hope you won't think I'm reneging on my duties, I have decided to take a step back and let Joseph take over more responsibilities of running the estate.' Joseph sat up and looked directly at his father. He couldn't believe it, but a lump came to his throat as he tried to control the tears that threatened his composure. For his father to do this, to entrust more of the running and decision making of the estate, was such a mark of trust, he was so utterly grateful and overwhelmed. 'Of course, I will always be on hand to help and advice when needed and will always be found in and around the Dower House, where my future wife and I intend living.'

This was another shock, and Emily and Joseph exchanged looks of surprise. 'But Father.......' Joseph started

'No buts. Shelagh and I would like to live somewhere smaller, and I know she would be happier pottering around her new garden, I think she already has plans for it! And besides, we hope it won't be too long before

The Hall is filled with lots of grandchildren, living and coming to stay, after all there are three of you young couples.' Much laughter followed this and few blushes spared. More champagne was called for and yet another announcement for Stanley the butler to take back to the kitchen, and for himself to despair yet again and wonder if it wasn't time for him to leave this household!

Over the next few weeks, Joseph received more instructions and guidance regarding the estate. Henry-Carmichael made appointments with his solicitor and bank manager to meet and discuss the changes with Joseph, and he was more than gratified how much interest and understanding Joseph took, even mentioning here and there where he thought improvements could be made which would not only benefit the estate, but the servants and tenants. His father was impressed as were the solicitor and bank manager.

The news of Lord Fanshaw's and Shelagh's betrothal was greeted by the servants and tenants of the estate, and most of the village, with pleasure, this could not be said of many of surrounding society, though by now many were of the attitude, well what could you expect after who his daughter and two sons had married! If any disapproval reached either sets of ears, it was quickly dismissed.

Eilish and Mirabelle were soon organising Shelagh in the area of her wardrobe and what she should wear as a June bride, but Shelagh would not be persuaded to wear anything she thought too young or unsuitable. Although the purchase of new clothes was a new one for her, Shelagh did agree to attend Mrs Wrights Emporium and discuss with her head seamstress, a suitable outfit for a woman of her age and a second marriage.

When Emily asked Henry-Carmichael what he had in mind for their wedding breakfast, he suggested she speak to Shelagh and then organise it with Cook and Mrs Green. Realising that his announcement had left Emily unsure of her situation at The Hall, he thought it only fair to make it clear that as he would shortly be leaving to live at the Dower House, Emily would be in charge of running The Hall. It would be her domain and with this in mind he decided to call all the servants together and make the situation clear to all. From now on, Emily was the Lady of the house, and any arrangements she wanted should be accepted.

He felt a little sorry for Emily as she sat beside him, listening to him inform the servants of the new regime, and thought it might be a good idea to make an informal suggestion, especially as Emily had little or no experience of dealing with servants.

'Might I suggest Emily that perhaps a little informal chat with various members of servants, when they can tell you what their currant duties are, may help you to understand and perhaps you may get a better idea for some changes you would like to implement?'

Emily smiled and agreed. 'Yes, I think that might be a good idea.' she replied looking round nervously at the faces that stared back her. After all, it wasn't that many weeks ago when she too had been servants, albeit a nurse-companion to Joseph, and now, here she was, Mistress of the house. She hoped there would be no animosity towards her, though there hadn't seemed to be so far.

Taking her father-in-law's advice, Emily set off one afternoon to visit Mrs McGovern, and was greeted warmly on arrival. Having told her about Henry-Carmichael's suggestion to talk to Shelagh regarding the wedding breakfast, Emily asked if she thought it would be a good idea to hold an informal meeting with Mrs Green and Cook to discuss the wedding breakfast and arrangements, over tea and cake? Shelagh thought it an excellent idea and together they agreed an afternoon.

Relieved that her suggestion had gone down so well, Emily returned to The Hall, and rang the bell for Mrs Green, who although surprised at the suggestion, did not take umbrage, and said she would note the day and time in her diary, and tell Cook to have some ideas to put forward.

In the evening, when they were alone, Emily discussed with Joseph her first steps to organising arrangements with servants, and that she was pleased at the reception she'd received. Joseph said he was surprised, although secretly relieved, as he pointed out to his new wife, she was a lovely lady and deserved to get the respect and love she deserved. That night when they made love, another little miracle took place.

That evening, as Rajiv poured over plans for the new house to be built in the grounds of the hospital, Mirabelle put her arms around him, playfully nibbling his neck.

'Would you behave yourself you naughty girl and tell me if there is anything else you think is required on these plans? As you see, I have designed it on the style of buildings we have in India. We call them bungalows, and they are all on one level, what do you think?' He asked

'I think they're amazing, I think you're amazing' Mirabelle replied playfully. It was obvious he was not going to get any sense out of her this evening, she was in a playful mood. He wondered if she would still be happy when he dropped the bombshell that their planned delayed honeymoon to India was to be delayed yet again.

'Dearest.' He turned to her, still seated, pulling her gently on to his lap. 'I hope you won't be too disappointed, but I fear we may have to delay our delayed honeymoon again. It's just that..' Raj got no further and to his surprise received a swift kiss on the lips and a hug as she buried her head into his shoulder and whispered in his ear.

'Just as well my love, it would not be good to go on such a long journey in my condition!' For a moment, the pair sat clasped together as if made of stone.

'What did you say?' He asked incredulously.

'I said.......'

'You are with child? He stated his face beaming with excitement and pride. 'Are you sure?'

'Well you're the doctor, so you tell me Doctor dearest.'

'How far do you think?'

'Two months possibly, I know it's early days but I read Miss Nightingales notes on this and I think I am definitely on my way towards motherhood. So what do you think of that, husband!'

Gently he enfolded her in his arms, stroking her from her head down to her back as though she were a fine piece of priceless porcelain, which of course, to him, she was.

'We will keep this secret to ourselves for a little while, perhaps announce it at your Fathers wedding, after all, wasn't he just saying he wanted grandchildren.'

Henry-Carmichael would laugh in a few months' time and wonder at the magic of his remark at Joseph and Emily's wedding.

In the cosy villa Teddy and Eilish called home, Teddy was thoughtful. 'Penny for them?' Eilish asked.

'Sorry?' Asked Teddy

'I said, Penny for them. Your thoughts. You seemed miles away.'

Teddy gave her a lazy smile and held out his hand to her. 'I was. I was thinking.'

'Am I allowed to know what about?'

'I was thinking about what my Papa said at Joseph' wedding.'

'Which bit? your Papa said quite a lot.' She answered laughing. Teddy raised an eyebrow smiling. 'He did didn't he, took us all by surprise. They were like a couple of naughty children, having kept a secret for so long then decided to own up. Still, good luck to them, why should they live alone and lonely when we've all got our loved ones.'

'Sooooo, was this what you were thinking about?'

'No. No, I was thinking about what he said about grandchildren, and wondered how you felt about that?'

'Oh Teddy, I would love to have a family with you.' Eilish said, tears of joy filling her eyes.

'Do you think we should?'

'Why not?'

'Well, these.' he said pointing to his withered legs.

'What's your legs got to do with it?' Eilish asked

'Well, what sort of a father would I make with these? I can't run around with them, I can't walk without my crutches or sticks....'

'There's more to being a father than being able to run around. You can still walk, ride a horse, but more importantly, you would give them love, and that's what every child wants and should have. You are a wonderful, kind, loving man. A man I'm proud to call my husband. Look at what you've achieved. You're educated, been to university, run a successful law practice and you've made me a very happy wife. So yes, I think we should have a family, lots and lots of children.'

Teddy laughed at her enthusiasm. 'Whoa there, hold on, lots and lots? How about one to be going on with?'

And it wasn't to be long before morning sickness took hold of Eilish and she could be heard to cry. 'If this is having a baby, there's only going to be one!'

CHAPTER 19

Friday June the twenty-first eighteen sixty-one. The day dawned sunny and warm and at six in the morning, Shelagh was sitting in the garden of the cottage she had lived in since arriving in Wynchampton on a cold winter's day many years before. She was reflecting on her life with its many twists and turns but despite everything, she'd had a good life and been lucky for so many reasons.

Despite the poverty she was born into in Ireland, she'd had wonderful, loving parents who'd done their best for her. She'd had a wonderful, loving husband in Cormac who'd given her two beautiful, hardworking, clever children, and when tragedy struck her little family, Cormac's amazing employer, Lord Fanshaw, had taken them under his wing. And now she was about to marry that very same man, her saviour. She would, for a time, be Lady Fanshaw, not that the title was of any importance to her, it was the man himself she had fallen in love with and who had fallen in love with her. And now, her beautiful daughter and son-in-law, were to give her the greatest gift, a grandchild, though it was early days and Shelagh was sworn to secrecy. The only reason she knew, was that she'd caught her daughter being sick on a recent visit, and poorly as she was, Eilish couldn't help confiding in her mother.

Today she would marry for the second time, only this time everything would be so different, not the love she felt for her future husband, no, not that, both men had been wonderful, strong, honest, hardworking, no this time the difference would be security, not that this was the reason for her acceptance, oh no. No, this time she wanted to show Henry the love he'd missed out on in his previous marriage. How she longed to make their remaining years together full of happiness.

'Mammy? What're you doing out here, aren't you cold?'

Shelagh looked up and across the garden where her son Eamon stood on the doorstep, rubbing his eyes with his fists to remove the sleep. Today, this handsome young son of hers would be giving his mammy away. She smiled at the name. Funny how no matter how many years they'd lived in England, certain traits of their Irishness remained, like her children still referring to her as Mammy, not Mother or Mama, but Mammy.

'No, I'm not cold. Just taking in this glorious sunny, peaceful morning.'

'Are you going to miss it here?' He asked.

Shelagh looked around thoughtfully. 'No, I don't think so. I'm looking forward to putting my mark on my new garden.'

Eamon laughed. 'So it was true, Henry said you'd already started making plans for it.'

'Yes, it was true, and less of the "Henry" from you, my lad. It's Papa or Father from now on.'

Eamon was thoughtful. It wasn't that he didn't like his future stepfather, somehow it just seemed a bit disloyal to his late Daddy. But then again, he had called him "Daddy" and it had all been so long ago, and let's be honest, hadn't Lord Fanshaw been like a father to him ever since his own daddy had died in that terrible accident? He sighed, he supposed in time he would get used to it, he would have to practice and in time it wouldn't sound so strange. As he went back indoors, he tried it out, 'Father, Papa, Father, Papa, Father Papa.' It still sounded strange.

Shelagh cooked breakfast for Eamon, the last she was likely to cook for him for some time, unless he visited the Dower House or changed his mind and came to live with them. He'd had the choice, but when he shyly asked if he could stay on at the cottage, Henry had generously said, if he really wanted to stay, then he would legally hand over the cottage to Eamon but once again telling him that should he ever want to join them in the Dower House, it would always be his home and he would be welcome.

At eleven on the dot, Shelagh heard a carriage pull up outside, and Eamon went to greet his sister and brother-in-law. Eilish was still looking a little peaky and Shelagh felt for the poor girl. Unfortunately, her mother was unable to know just how debilitating this situation could be, having been lucky enough never to have suffered from it with either

her two confinements. She smiled as she watched Teddy tenderly helping his wife down from the carriage.

Running downstairs, Shelagh ran into the kitchen to pour a glass of ginger cordial she'd made from a recipe one of the women in the village had given her. She'd been assured this was good for all sorts of ailments but particularly morning sickness. Shelagh smiled to herself at the memory at the way the woman had looked her up and down until she'd burst out laughing and explained' 'Oh no, it's not for me, it's for the daughter of a friend of mine she lied. She did not wish it to be known it was for Eilish before the rest of the family were aware.

As Eilish sipped the drink, she gradually felt her stomach settle and asked her mother if she could take the bottle with her.

When Shelagh came downstairs, ready to go to her wedding, they all gasped. Tears sprang to Eilish's eyes and even Teddy and Eamon were choked with emotion. Her dress and jacket were of a pale blue/grey satin with a matching hat. It was unfussy but stylish and elegant, she looked every bit the Lady she was about to become.

In a vase on the table, Shelagh withdrew a small bouquet of blue, white and purple flowers which had arrived the previous day from Henry. She stood beaming at them. 'Well, shall we go?'

They took a slow trot through the village, partly so as not to jolt Eilish too much but also so that those villagers, who were not able to attend the wedding, could wave her off, wishing her good luck, and get a look at her outfit.

On this occasion, the chapel was packed. Apart from their family, all the servants had been invited, with the added bonus that although Cook had been in charge of the menu, his Lordship had engaged outside waiters and footmen to serve and be in attendance, this enabled the servants to sit down and thoroughly enjoy the celebrations with the new Lady Fanshaw. Only one person declined this kind invitation and that was sent with the RSVP attached to the notice, informing his Lordship that Mr Harold Stanley, butler, would be leaving his Lordships employment at the end of the quarter.

Although angry at Stanley's rude rebuff, Henry-Carmichael later thought his butler's action for the best and informed Joseph and Emily they should start looking for a replacement. Perhaps a younger less stringent person may be sought for the post.

Shelagh had also invited some special friends she'd made in the village, and this included Mr and Mrs Wright from the Emporium. Several of the tenant farmers and their families were also invited, though not all could attend the wedding breakfast, as farm work had to take precedence. But they were enthusiastic and eager to cram into the tiny chapel on the day to take part in the nuptials.

Henry-Carmichael had a little chuckle at what was supposed to be a quiet and private gathering. As he looked around at the assorted people gathered and compared it to his first wedding which had included the cream of society, it seemed a happier and gayer gathering this time.

As the cords of the organ struck the music of the wedding march, which had become popular when Mendelssohn had written it in eighteen forty-two, Henry turned to watch as Eamon sedately walked his Mother down the aisle, into the hands of her future husband.

The service was a simple one, prayers were said, and hymns sung by the country folk with much gusto and without inhibitions as to who could sing and who couldn't!

When returning to The Hall, it was not only the bride and groom awaiting their guests, but the whole family lined up to shake hands. It amused Eilish and Emily, that they were curtsied too as their guests arrived. Shelagh was glad of this support as she was sure she would have felt uncomfortable without it.

By the time the gong sounded for them to enter the great dining room, servants, villagers, and those tenants that had been able to make it, looked around in wonder. Of course the servants had often seen the room in all its glory, but never as a guest so it took on a whole new feel for them, and they were as proud as punch to think they worked for such an amazing employer.

The bride and groom were leaving as soon as their wedding breakfast was over as he was taking Shelagh on a surprise visit to Scotland where they would be staying with an old friend of Henry-Carmichael, in his Scottish Castle. He announced that on their return, they would be moving into the Dower House, and therefore he was handing over to Joseph and Emily to look after the guests and ensure everyone enjoyed the rest of the day and evening.

Whilst Eilish helped her mother out of her wedding outfit and into her travelling clothes, she confided in her that Teddy was in the study with his father giving him the news of a future little
Fanshaw. Unbeknown to them, Teddy wasn't the only one!

'Father, before you leave, might I have a word?' Joseph called out as his father headed towards his study. Henry-Carmichael paused, turning to see his son and Emily running towards him. 'Don't look so worried Papa, we have news for you, good news and didn't want you to leave before we'd told you.' Intrigued, Henry held open the study door to usher them inside. Just as he was about to close it, Teddy, Mirabelle and Rajiv, followed in their footsteps.

'Papa! We must speak with you, it's urgent.' Called out Mirabelle dragging poor Rajiv in her wake.

'And I too need to speak with you.' Teddy called. 'It really cannot wait.'

'Neither can my news.' Mirabelle said stamping her foot impatiently.

'Well you'd better all come in, unless anything any of you have to say is of a private nature?'

They all spoke at once that no, their news concerned the rest of the family. Mystified, he looked from one to another, as did they. 'Well, as Joseph spoke first perhaps he would like to tell me what the problem is?'

Joseph relaxed, and still holding Emily's hand he looked at her and then his father. 'Papa, Father, you know you said when you announced you would be leaving The Hall to live in the Dower House, well you mentioned grandchildren.' Henry frowned. 'Well Emily and I will be producing the next generation of Fanshaw's in January next year!' He announced with a flourish, beaming at his wife, brother, sister and brother-in-law.

'Oh!' Came from Mirabelle whose mouth dropped open in amazement, whilst Henry, when the news sank in, congratulated Joseph and Emily with the shaking of hands and hugs for Emily and followed by the rest of the family. Henry was thrilled.

'Why that's the most wonderful news, the best since you gave me the news you wanted to marry, congratulations both of you.'

....Mirabelle was laughing fit to bust. 'Oh my goodness, I'm so pleased for you.' She turned and took the hand of her husband. 'But I'm sorry to disappoint you brother, but I'm afraid Raj and I have beaten you to it, our little one is arriving in November.'

'What!' they all shrieked. Then Teddy was roaring with laughter. They all turned.

'And ours is due next February! Well there you go Father, you said you wanted to fill the house, and as Mirabelle and I are twins, what are the chances of one of us producing a pair? Hm, what do you think Raj?'

'Well I hope it's Eilish!' Raj replied, then having received a playful punch from his wife he added. 'Joking, the more the merrier.'

They decided that as Teddy and Joseph' arrivals were not until the following year, they would keep it in the family for now. But Henry couldn't wait to tell Shelagh the news, he knew she would make a fabulous Grandmama.

EPILOGUE

The journey to Castle Campbell, where Henry and Shelagh were to spend two weeks at the invitation of Lord Andrew Campbell, would take several days. Henry planned to make two stops, one to see a little of the city of York and the surrounding countryside, the other at Gretna Green, famous for offering marriages for underage and runaway couples.

When they left The Hall it was with the excitement of not only their new life together, but also with the news of at least three grandchildren on the way.

Their future looked exciting and although Shelagh was looking forward to staying in a Scottish castle high up in the Highlands, she was also eager for her return where she could take up life with her new husband, awaiting the arrival of three new babies and who knew, maybe more.

She looked forward to seeing Eamon go forward with the new position recently offered, working with the equine veterinary, who regularly attended Henry's stables. With the possibility he may one day get to university to study, Joe Blackstone the blacksmith, had been particularly good about Eamon's new career choice and they had compromised with Eamon working part-time with him and Danny O'Hara the vet.

Life! From poverty to a Lady, who would have thought it? And now, what did the future have in store? She wasn't sure but glancing at Henry, she knew it was going to be good for the new Lord and Lady Fanshaw of Wynchampton Hall.

Printed in Great Britain
by Amazon